Meg was suddenly very aware of their positions again. Of how little distance separated them.

She would have to lean forward only a few inches and she could kiss him....

And she wanted to. So much it shocked her. So much she felt herself actually move in. Barely. But some...

Did he move, too? Upward? Toward her?

If he did it was so scant she couldn't be sure. But he might have...

Did that mean it would be all right for her to kiss him? That he might even want her to?

She wanted to.

She really, really wanted to....

But what made her hesitate was reminding herself that Logan *was* her boss. That he was Tia's dad. That that wasn't a complication she needed right now.

Dear Reader,

To me, the small town of Northbridge, Montana, is a safe haven, a good place to regroup. And that's what it is to Meg Perry, too. She's had something frightening happen to her and it's left her shaken. So spending the summer back in her hometown, being nanny to an adorable three-year-old, seems like the best way for her to get back in touch with the kind of joy and fun she's found in working with kids in the past.

For Logan McKendrick, Northbridge is a way to simplify a life that's become complicated, and concentrate on being a single dad. The fact that Logan and Meg discover each other in the process just happens. But when it does, it happens with a great big bang that I think is fun to watch. I hope you will, too.

As always, happy reading!

Best,

Victoria Pade

MARRYING THE NORTHBRIDGE NANNY

VICTORIA PADE

Silhouette®

SPECIAL EDITION®

Published by Silhouette Books

America's Publisher of Contemporary Romance

SILHOUETTE BOOKS

ISBN-13: 978-0-373-65519-9

Recycling programs
for this product may
not exist in your area.

MARRYING THE NORTHBRIDGE NANNY

Printed in U.S.A.

VICTORIA PADE

is an author of both romance and mystery novels. She lives in a suburb of Denver, Colorado, with her two daughters, Cori and Erin, and her schnauzer, Charlie. When she isn't writing she's experimenting with recipes for anything chocolate and trying hard to learn to cook something that isn't dessert.

Chapter One

It was a sunny Saturday afternoon in mid-June when Meg Perry arrived at the home of Logan McKendrick. Sunny and warm and quiet—the day had a lazy feel to it. And yet Meg felt anything but the kind of laid-back, calm composure that should have gone with a day like that. She was wound up and fighting butterflies in her stomach as she stopped her car engine.

She took a deep breath and a quick glance at herself in her rearview mirror, trying to chase away some of those butterflies.

She'd pulled her wavy red hair back into a professional-looking French twist. She'd used only a slight dusting of blush to give her pale skin some color, a few swipes of mascara so her green eyes didn't look washed out, and a pale lip gloss just as a finishing touch.

Presentable, not flashy—that had been her goal and she was satisfied that she'd accomplished it. But it still didn't help her unwind.

Analyzing her tension, she didn't think it should have come from meeting-new-people-jitters since she knew the McKendrick family. At least she knew them the way everyone in her small hometown of Northbridge, Montana, knew even people they weren't close to—she knew *of* them. Or she had, ten years ago before she'd left Northbridge to go to college. But they didn't seem to qualify as strangers, so meeting them shouldn't have been causing her stress.

The butterflies in her stomach also shouldn't have come from feeling on edge about the job interview she was there for when the discussion was only to confirm the terms of her employment as nanny to Logan McKendrick's three-year-old daughter. A position that Logan's sister Hadley had essentially hired her for on the phone because Meg's credentials were far and away more than any nanny needed—she had a Ph.D. in child psychology and was on sabbatical from Children's Hospital in Denver after four years of work that had been considerably more complicated than nannying.

But the butterflies were flitting around anyway and she supposed they were just another part of the residual effects of The Incident—or what everyone referred to as *The Incident*. She'd been easy to rattle since then. Which was part of why she was there…

She got out of the car and brushed the lines out of her beige linen slacks, making sure her cream-colored camp shirt was tucked in. Then she headed for the two-story farmhouse that was sporting a fresh coat of yellow paint trimmed in white.

As she climbed the steps onto the wide front porch, she could see through the screen that the front door was open. But there were no signs of life inside, so she pushed the button for the doorbell. It didn't make a sound. Maybe she hadn't pushed it hard enough. She tried again. But again, no sound.

She was five minutes early, but she knew Logan and Hadley were expecting her.

She tried the doorbell a third time.

"It dudn't work," came a quiet little voice just before two puppies appeared from behind the open front door inside.

Meg glanced downward to discover a very small child barely peeking at her from behind that same door.

Big brown eyes peered at her warily and beyond those a pair of Spiderman swim goggles that the child was wearing on her forehead, the little girl was hidden behind the door.

"Hi," Meg greeted in her most inviting tone of voice. "I'm Meg. I'll bet you're Tia." The three-year-old she was to be nanny to.

The little girl's only response was a timid nod of her head of curly blond hair. It was cut short and caplike but not so short that the curls didn't bounce with the nod.

"Are you swimming today?" Meg asked because of the goggles, thinking that maybe a pool had been added to the old Ludwig farm at some point and that maybe that was where Logan and Hadley were.

But Tia gave a negative shake of her head in answer to that, offering nothing more and ducking coyly behind the door, completely out of sight.

The dogs were wrestling with each other in the doorway, growling playfully. Meg hunkered down as if they were what she was really interested in, knowing that while a three-year-old was naturally shy with strangers, they didn't like sharing the spotlight and that that might help draw Tia out again.

"Oh, aren't you two the cutest things. Come over here and see me…."

The puppies stopped their wrestling and came noses first to the screen, tails wagging, eager for her attention.

"Hello. Hello, you little sweethearts," she cooed to them.

As Meg had anticipated, Tia reappeared from behind the door, even coming farther out than she'd been before. Far enough for Meg to see her round, rosy cheeks and the long eyelashes that fanned her big brown eyes. Far enough for Meg to see that she was wearing a Spiderman costume to go with the goggles.

"Those are my dogs Max and Harry," she said.

"Max and Harry," Meg repeated, still focusing on the puppies. "I don't know what kind of dogs you are, Max and Harry, but you're just babies, aren't you?" she cooed some more.

"Max is a doodle and Harry is a re-doodle," Tia informed her, still timidly but with some authority, finally coming to stand in the doorway with the dogs.

Meg wasn't sure what doodles were, let alone *re*-doodles. But the information was coming from a three-year-old, so she doubted it was reliable.

"And you're Spiderman today," Meg said, aiming her attention at Tia again, who seemed more ready to accept it.

"I'm Spider*girl*," Tia corrected.

Meg nodded. "Now that I look again, I can see that. Spidergirl—of course. Well, Spidergirl, I'm here to talk to your dad and your aunt Hadley," she told Tia. "Could you get one of them for me?"

"Tia? Where are you and what are you up to?" came a woman's voice just then. A split second later, the woman herself appeared at the opposite end of the hallway that ran from the front door, alongside a staircase leading to the upper level, to the kitchen in the rear of the house.

"Oh! We didn't know someone was here," the woman said when she spotted Meg. "Is that you, Meg?" she asked as she hurried to the door.

"It is," Meg confirmed.

Because the hallway was dim and there was bright sunshine in the kitchen, the woman was in silhouette until she reached the entry. But even then Meg didn't recognize her. She had not been Logan's or Hadley McKendrick's contemporary growing up. At twenty-nine, Meg was six years younger than Logan and four years younger than Hadley, and with an age gap like that, none of them had had any reason to take notice of each other. Add to that the facts that Meg hadn't been close friends with any of Logan's and Hadley's younger half siblings, that both Logan and Hadley had left Northbridge when they'd graduated high school, and they really were virtual strangers except that Meg and Hadley had recently spoken on the telephone about the nanny position.

So, when the other woman reached the front door, Meg said, "And you must be Hadley," to make sure. Besides, not only had she and Hadley McKendrick not been friends, not only had more than a decade gone by since they'd even seen each other, but the Hadley McKendrick Meg had any recollection of at all was very heavy and the woman who came to the door was anything but.

"Yes, it's me," Hadley answered with a laugh. "I know, I'm half the woman I used to be—almost literally. I lost a hundred pounds."

"That's quite an accomplishment," Meg marveled.

Hadley pulled the puppies out of the way and opened the door as Tia looked on from the sidelines again. "Come on in. We didn't know you were here."

"The doorbell—"

"Oh, I know, it needs to be replaced. I should have warned you but I forgot about it."

Meg went into the entryway and Hadley latched the screen door behind her. Then to her niece, Hadley said, "Tia, your daddy is in the backyard. Go get him and tell him Meg is here."

"I'm Spidergirl," Tia insisted.

"Okay, Spidergirl, go get your dad," Hadley amended.

Very seriously, as if she were about to take flight, Tia lowered the goggles over her eyes and then ran down the hallway Hadley had come from. But at the same moment Tia reached the opposite end of it, a tall man appeared there, too, and the three-year-old crashed into him.

Because of the silhouette effect caused by the lighting, the most Meg could tell about the scene in the distance was that the tall man weathered the blow and scooped the little girl into his arms to carry her back with him.

"Hi," he called as he did.

Meg assumed he was Logan McKendrick. She barely recognized him, too, when she got her first clear view of him as he joined them in the entryway. He hadn't had the kind of transformation his sister had, but Meg didn't recall him being so staggeringly handsome, either.

Broad shoulders and a lean muscular body went with the height that was at least an inch over six foot. His hair was a shiny walnut-brown that he wore slightly long with the top swept to one side and sideburns that were a sexy fraction of an inch longer than Meg was used to, too. He had perfectly peaked lips, a straight nose, and translucent, pale, pale blue eyes that were so mesmerizing that it took Meg a moment to stop staring at them and realize he'd suggested that they go into the living room.

"So you're Meg Perry," he said when they had, motioning for Meg to sit on the rocking chair across the coffee table while Hadley sat on the tweed sofa. He took up the other end of couch, settling Tia on his jean-clad lap so she could rest back against his yellow polo shirt.

"Yes, I'm Meg Perry."

He was studying her closely, and being under the scrutiny of those remarkable eyes that had an almost ethereal quality to them made the butterflies take wing in her stomach again.

Then he said, "I remember your brother Jared—he was a year older than me—"

"And I was the same age as your brother Noah," Hadley put in.

"But other than that," Logan took up where his sister had left off, "I only have a faint recollection of two red-headed Perry girls."

"Kate and I both have red hair. We're the youngest of the four kids," Meg contributed. "And don't feel bad, I can't say I honestly remember you two, either."

"So we start fresh," Logan decreed.

"Sounds good to me," Meg answered.

With that settled, Logan said, "From what Hadley told me about you, there's no question that you can do the job—you have a doctorate in child psychology?"

"Right." Meg could see that that left him wondering why she was there for a nanny job, so she tried to avoid any questions she might not want to answer and said, "I'm just taking a little time away from it to have the summer back home."

That kept him from digging any deeper. "And Hadley checked your references—you come with nothing but high praise, so I can't see that there's anything for me to worry about with you. I'm thinking that maybe I should just give you an idea of what I want on this end and you can decide if it's a job you're willing to spend your time doing."

"Okay," Meg agreed, wishing she wasn't finding it so difficult to concentrate. And she didn't understand why she was. She talked to parents all the time—even some who were notably attractive—and she'd never had any problem. But for some reason she just kept getting lost in looking at Logan McKendrick, at comparing the man he was now with the boy she barely remembered and judging him somehow so much better looking.

Stop it! she told herself firmly, glancing at Tia for a moment's diversion as the little girl raised the goggles to her forehead again, climbed from her father's lap and went to tease the puppies with a chew toy.

"We bought this place because it gave us housing, workspace, a showroom and some future expansion possibilities all in one," was the first thing that Meg actually heard again. "That means that we'll be living, working and running our business from here, but I still want it to be a relaxed, family atmosphere."

Meg knew that Logan McKendrick and Chase Mackey—another Northbridge native—were the Mackey and McKendrick of Mackey and McKendrick Furniture Designs, and that that was the business he was talking about.

"Of course Tia's safety is important," he was saying. "In all the usual ways, but I also don't like to have her around the workshop when any of the equipment is being used—a lot of our tools and equipment and machinery are dangerous to her. So you'll have to make sure she doesn't get away from you."

"Absolutely," Meg said.

"I don't expect you to be the maid, so you don't have to worry about household chores—although if you wanted to set up Tia's room for me, I'd count that as a huge favor. I still haven't been able to get all of her stuff out of the moving boxes."

"And I *need* Grilla," Tia added from the floor, obviously listening even as she played with the dogs.

"*Grilla* is her stuffed gorilla," Logan McKendrick explained. "He has to be in that room somewhere but—"

Meg smiled. "I love to organize. I'd be happy to set up Tia's room and maybe we can find *Grilla* together."

"That'd be fantastic," he said as if it took a burden off him. "I'd also like for this to be a sort of communal living arrangement."

Alarms went off in the reserved Meg. "Communal-living arrangement?" she repeated, wondering what exactly he was suggesting. She knew next to nothing personal about this man or his sister. They could have gone out into the world and become some kind of freaks....

"Hadley said I'd have an apartment separate from where you live," Meg added.

For some reason, her qualms made Logan McKendrick smile a small, one-sided smile that didn't alleviate her concerns because although it was appealing and made him all the more handsome, there was also a devilish quality to it.

"Did your whole body just clench up?" he asked with a laugh.

"Logan!" his sister chastised.

"Well, it's true," he said.

Meg didn't wait for Hadley to say more. She just went on, trying a different tack. "What do you mean by communal living?"

"Not the same thing you do," he said, his tone intimating that she had a dirty mind. Then, as if he were the poster boy for innocence while still obviously enjoying the discomfort he'd caused her, he continued. "Yes, you'll have an apartment separate from the house—in the top half of the garage. I just finished it, as a matter of fact, so you'll be the first to use it. What I mean by *communal living* is that I'd like for this not to be only a nine-to-five job. I'd like for you to become someone Tia sees as part of the family—remember, I said I wanted a *relaxed, family* atmosphere?"

"As long as *relaxed, family atmosphere* doesn't mean kissing cousins," she muttered.

"We aren't cousins and I promise—no kissing," he responded to her utterance, somehow making her feel the teensiest bit rejected for some reason that didn't make any sense.

But Meg ignored it and got back on track herself. "Relaxing a little is my goal this summer, too," she said, just more stiffly than she wished it had come out.

And that made the crooked smile straighten and broaden into a full grin. "You're the old Reverend's granddaughter, aren't you?" he asked out of the blue then, as if light had just dawned in him to explain her behavior. And, to some degree, Meg's being the former town reverend's granddaughter did throw light on her reaction.

"Yes," she confirmed.

He nodded slowly, knowingly, and in a way she wasn't sure she appreciated because she could see that he was thinking she was some prim and proper, stuffy, nose-in-the-air conservative prig like her grandfather. And she wasn't. She was just a very quiet person who battled shyness along with the lingering effects of a stringent upbringing.

He didn't pursue that reference to the Reverend, though, finally continuing with what he'd been saying. "I want this to be an informal environment for us all. Casual, friendly…"

Did he think she was going to be *un*friendly? Or was she just giving the impression that she was too wooden? Because she knew she sometimes came off that way even though she tried not to.

In an attempt to counteract that impression, she said, "One of the main reasons I want to do this is for the fun of it. I like the idea of Tia seeing me as part of the family. But all kids need boundaries, limitation, rules and to know what the expectations of them are. It not only teaches them things, it also makes them feel safe. So, as Tia's nanny—assuming you decide to give me the job—I'll make sure there are enough of those."

While Meg's intention had been to ease Logan McKendrick's mind, by the end of that all the amusement had left his handsome face and a slight frown had replaced it. "What are we talking in the way of boundaries, limitations, rules and expectations?"

"Nothing out of the ordinary," she tried to reassure him. "Regular bedtimes and mealtimes, making sure teeth are brushed, hair is combed, that she's dressed when she should be. She can be given small responsibilities like helping to pick up her toys, putting shoes in the closet—age-appropriate expectations. Three-year-olds like to test authority, to see what they can get away with, what they can control, and just how independent they can be—some of that is good and needs to be encouraged, some of it has to be struggled against. She can learn that there is a right and a wrong time and place for certain things. Punishments can include brief time-outs, maybe going without dessert—"

"Okay, I can see you know your stuff," Logan said to stop her.

Had she sounded too clinical? Sometimes she did that, too. Unintentionally.

Still in damage-control-mode, she said, "But three-year-olds primarily need a lot of playtime, a lot of safe ways to explore their environments…" She stopped herself this time, knowing she was still sounding too much like a textbook. "And really, beyond doing what needs to be done to keep her safe and happy, I would just want her to have a good time."

Logan McKendrick nodded but she could see that he had more reservations now than he'd had before.

"We don't keep military precision when it comes to meals," he said. "I give Tia breakfast whenever she gets up in the morning, lunches will probably just be you and Tia because Hadley and I will be working, but we like to do dinner as a group project with everyone pitching in—even Tia gets out the napkins—and then we sit down to eat together. How would you feel about that? Would you want to be included or not?"

"I'd like to be included. Actually, family dinners are more important than some people think."

"But again, it's a *casual* thing—the cooking, the cleanup, we all just chat while we get things ready, while we eat."

"It sounds great," Meg said, deciding to keep her answers more simple. "I don't know how good a cook I am, but I know my way around a kitchen."

"We're not gourmets," Hadley assured.

"I should warn you, though," Meg said to Logan then, thinking that if she'd put him off too much maybe she should give him an easy way out of hiring her. "This is only a temporary thing for me. I'm on a leave-of-absence for the summer."

"Yeah, Hadley told me. But that's not a problem. We're just setting up in Northbridge again ourselves—in fact I've been so busy around here that I haven't even been into town more than a few times the whole month that Hadley and I have been here. I'm not sure what I'll want to do with Tia in the long run—the summer will give me a chance to check out the day care and pre-school situations."

"Playing with other kids is important, too—good social skills are something she'll need."

"I was thinking more along the lines of friends and playmates than *social skills*," Logan McKendrick said, and again Meg knew that something about her expertise actually seemed to rub him the wrong way.

Then he proved it and said, "I just want to be clear—Tia is a normal three-year-old kid who needs someone to look after her when I can't. She doesn't need a shrink."

"Oh, no, I understand that you aren't hiring me as a psychologist and that's actually why I want the job, so you don't have to worry about me being anything but her nanny."

He studied her with those pale blue eyes for a while

as if he was deciding if he could believe that. But after a moment he said, "I trust Hadley's judgment. If you want the job, it's yours. As long as you keep in mind that we're not fussy around here. This isn't a hospital or a classroom—it's home."

"Honestly, that's just what I want."

He took another long look at her, possibly deciding if he believed that, too. But then he said, "Okay, how about if you move in sometime tomorrow—"

"I have a wedding shower for my sister, Kate, tomorrow. Can I come in the evening, when it's over?"

"Sure. Anytime is fine. Then you can start on Monday."

"Actually, if I get here before Tia goes to bed tomorrow night maybe I can go through the bedtime routine with you so I know what that is?"

"That's fine, too. We *do* have a bedtime routine," he added as if he felt the need to convince her that not everything was unstructured, in case she was judging him.

"Do you want to see the apartment?" Hadley offered.

"I would but I have to go with Kate to do some wedding things. I'm sure it'll be fine," she said, making an attempt to sound more laid-back because she thought there was some judgment being passed by him, too. More laid-back than she actually was.

But she honestly didn't have more time to spend at this, so she said, "In fact, unless you have anything else you want to talk about, I should get going."

"No, feel free," Logan said.

"Harry piddled," Tia announced to the room in general then.

Hadley jumped up to scold the puppy and put him

outside, saying as she did, "I'll clean this, Logan, if you want to walk Meg out."

As Logan and Meg both got to their feet and headed for the front door, Logan said, "The puppies were Hadley's moving-here present to Tia so she's working the hardest to house-train them—it gets me out of a lot."

Meg laughed but she didn't know what to say. Sticking with the dog theme, she said, "Tia said Max is a doodle and Harry is a re-doodle, but I didn't know what she meant."

"Max is half poodle, half Labrador—a Labra-Doodle. Harry is half poodle, half golden retriever. He's a Golden-Doodle, but when we got them I made a joke about Max being a doodle and Harry being a re-doodle. Tia took it seriously."

That made Meg laugh, too.

Logan unlatched and opened the screen door then, holding it for her as she went out and going as far as the porch himself.

But for some reason, once she'd gone down the porch steps, Meg felt the need to pause, glance back, and reassure him. "I really do just want to be the nanny this summer."

He nodded. "I hope so," he said with what sounded like some skepticism.

She knew that there was nothing she could do from there but prove to him that she meant what she said, so she merely added, "I'll see you all tomorrow night."

"We'll be here."

They exchanged goodbyes and Meg went the rest of the way to her car, thinking that he didn't need to feel skeptical. Putting herself back in touch with the basics of happy, healthy kids—that's what she'd set out to do for the summer and that was all she intended to do.

As she started her car and put it into gear she realized that Logan McKendrick was still standing on the porch watching her go.

And just that quick it wasn't Tia or any other kids she was thinking about. It was the way he filled out a pair of jeans that struck her.

That certainly wasn't what she needed to be thinking about this summer!

But surely it would become old stuff the longer she was around him, the more she got used to seeing him.

At least she was counting on that being the case.

And she hoped that the casual, friendly, free-and-easy environment he was asking her to be a part of bred that familiarity in a hurry.

So she could stop even noticing the way he looked in jeans or anything else.

So she could stop noticing him at all…

Chapter Two

While Tia napped on Sunday afternoon, Hadley stayed to listen for her as Logan put the finishing touches on the apartment he'd promised to Meg Perry.

It was in the upper level of the triple-car garage close behind—but not attached to—his house. He'd hired out the plumbing, electrical, and drywalling work he wasn't qualified to do, but he'd done the rest of the construction himself.

The studio apartment wasn't as spacious as the loft that he and his partner were putting into the upper level of the barn. That would be Chase's place over the workroom, the office, and the showroom that were on the ground floor of that larger structure. But even so, the nanny's apartment was open and airy and not at all cramped.

There was a small kitchen with a built-in table that

Logan had designed, complete with a semi-ornate, hand-carved edge. The living room was comprised of a flat-screen TV hung on one wall in front of a sofa and two matching easy chairs that had come from a collection he and Chase had done a few years ago that were a combination of oak and leather that made them comfortable and sophisticated at once. There was a beautiful double-sized sleigh bed that Logan had also designed and made himself, set on a platform area that rose two steps above the rest of the space to give some sense of separation. And there was a large bathroom and walk-in closet that provided the only closed-in sections of the place.

Curtains had been hung, the hardwood floor was finished, and there was even a small fireplace with a mantel he'd crafted himself.

And as he stood surveying his handiwork to make sure the apartment was ready for occupancy, he was satisfied with the way it had come out. He was also a little turned on by the image of Meg Perry living there, using the table, sitting on the sofa and the easy chairs, sleeping in the bed.

And he had no idea why…

But then he wasn't quite sure what to make of Meg Perry all the way around. Or of his own reaction to her and the fact that he'd been thinking about her incessantly since she'd left yesterday.

Meg's sister, Kate—who lived in Northbridge—had seen an ad they had placed in the local newspaper and passed it along to Meg. She looked good on the surface—she had a Ph.D. in child psychology, for crying out loud, and Hadley had told him that she'd learned through their interview that Meg had gone from baby-sitting as a teenager to working her way through college doing day care, to counseling and treating kids at Children's Hospital in Denver. Her background was full of work with children, so who better to be Tia's nanny?

That had been Hadley's argument in favor of Meg since Hadley had handled that whole thing while he was juggling keeping up with the business, the move, and getting the apartment finished. So even though he'd been concerned that Meg Perry was tremendously over-qualified and wondered why she was willing to spend her summer as a nanny—something he still didn't have an answer to—Hadley had talked him into it.

His first impression of Meg hadn't been bad, but that had been surface, too. Initially, when he'd seen her standing at the other end of the hallway, he'd registered incredible, thick, wavy hair the color of cherrywood, beautiful emerald green eyes, and a warm smile.

By the time he'd joined her and Hadley in the entryway he'd realized that those weren't her only note-worthy physical attributes—she also had flawless alabaster skin; a perfect, straight, thin nose; high cheek-bones any model would have envied, and lips that he couldn't help thinking of as anything but luscious—although that didn't seem like a good way to think about his daughter's nanny.

She also had a great, compact, curvy little body.

But it hadn't only been her looks that had counted in her favor during that first impression. He'd also liked that she hadn't gone overboard trying to sweet-talk Tia the way he'd seen babysitters and other child-care givers do in an attempt to prove how good they were with kids. As a rule, once his back was turned, those were the people who ended up being the worst with her.

Meg Perry had been more on the conservative side than the effusive one, and he knew from experience that Tia responded better to being left to her own timetable when it came to letting new people in. That they were all better off with someone calm, soft-spoken, even-keeled.

Those were all things that had seemed to describe Meg Perry.

She'd also seemed slightly self-contained and maybe a little tense about coming into a new situation, but the warmth in her smile had led him to believe that there was a softer side to her that they'd probably see more of later on.

Then she'd trotted out that stuff about *age-appropriate expectations, social skills,* and *exploring the environment,* and that had made him think twice about her.

Tia was three years old, for crying out loud—he was lucky that she was out of diapers and eating the same foods he did. He needed someone to watch her, play with her, feed her, and keep her out of harm's way. He didn't need a bunch of textbook terms thrown at him. Besides, people who were convinced they knew so much more than anyone else that they had to educate lesser mortals struck a particularly raw nerve in him.

At that point he'd thought that maybe he shouldn't hire her.

On the other hand, he'd also known that Hadley was all for Meg Perry. And he'd gotten kind of a kick out of giving her a hard time for that communal-living panic she'd shown—kind of a kick that he hadn't felt in a long while. Plus he'd liked that hint of spunk she'd shown in the kissing-cousins comment.

And she did have that hair and those eyes…

He'd opted to give her the benefit of the doubt because Hadley had been so impressed by more than her résumé, because Hadley had liked her and had said that despite leaving Northbridge the way he and Chase and Hadley herself had, Meg still seemed like a North-bridge girl…

He and Chase and Hadley had all returned to their small hometown because they were weary of what they'd found in more bustling parts of the country—or, in Hadley's case, in more bustling parts of the world. They all wanted the homier atmosphere of Northbridge. The closeness. The down-to-earth aspects of it. And if that was what Meg Perry could offer Tia, then Hadley was right and Meg was the best person for the nanny job.

And it *was* a temporary situation, he reminded himself as he smoothed the quilt on the bed Hadley had made up for Meg.

Meg had made sure he knew she wasn't signing on for anything permanent but that could be his escape clause, too, if she ended up rubbing him wrong more than she rubbed him right.

Not that there would be any *rubbing* involved, he amended his own thoughts when more literal images of that began to pop into his mind. More literal and appeal-ing images…

But he wasn't interested in Meg Perry as anything but

Tia's nanny. Not only did he need to get settled into Northbridge again, but he also had to put his divorce behind him once and for all, and to concentrate on being a single dad. And even if he were in the market for a relationship—which he absolutely wasn't—it wouldn't be with a woman like Meg. That Ph.D. she was sporting, the expertise she hadn't been able to keep from spouting—those were like detour signs telling him to go in a different direction to avoid the kind of problems he'd encountered before. No matter how attractive Meg Perry might be, the last thing he wanted was another brain-meets-brawn situation with any woman.

And yet, even as he was telling himself that, he was standing at the foot of the sleigh bed picturing Meg Perry stretched out on the mattress…

It was that red hair, those eyes, the warmth in that smile that he just couldn't get out of his head…

But those things aside, he was betting that Miss Age-Appropriate-Expectations would probably not be able to resist showing off some more and that would hammer out of him whatever it was that had caused him to even dream about her last night.

At least that was what he was hoping.

Logan took his hand off the bed frame and jammed it into his jeans pocket.

Age-appropriate expectations. Social skills. Exploring the environment…

Those were the kinds of things he needed to remember about her. Not how green her eyes were. Not how soft her skin had looked. Not that when he'd joined her in the entryway he'd caught a whiff of a clean, airy wildflower scent that he knew hadn't come from his sister or his daughter.

Meg Perry was the nanny and that was it. Yes, he'd meant it when he'd told her he wanted her to be a part of everything around here so she seemed like family, but that was for Tia's sake, not his.

He just needed to think of her the way he thought of his ex-wife—as a person he had to be civil and courteous to for his daughter's happiness and well-being.

Other than that?

There wouldn't *be* anything other than that between him and Meg Perry.

It was something he swore to himself.

That no matter what, her brain was not meeting his brawn.

"You yike it?"

It took Meg a split second to translate *yike*. She'd arrived at the McKendrick home just after Tia's bath, in time for the bedtime story. Logan was perched on Tia's small twin bed, his daughter by his side as he read *Goodnight Moon* to her. Meg was on the rocking chair near the bed and the moment Logan finished the book, Tia leaned forward to see Meg—whom she was only beginning to acknowledge—to ask that question.

Yike was apparently *like*—did she *like* the book that Logan had read?

"I did," Meg assured the little girl.

"You din't say guh'night moon," Tia accused.

At the end of the story, after Logan had read the last line, bidding good-night to noises everywhere, Tia had added, "Good night, moon," and Logan had repeated it. Meg hadn't.

So she did now. "Good night, moon."

That seemed to satisfy the three-year-old because she sat back against her pillow again.

Logan threw Meg a smile that crinkled the corners of his striking eyes. She'd lectured herself since she'd left here yesterday that she wasn't going to notice things like that. But there it was anyway.

Then, to his daughter, he said, "Tell me what I told you happens tomorrow."

"You and An' Had has to work."

"And while we work, who will be here with you?"

Tia leaned forward again, pointed a finger at Meg, and said, "Her will."

"Meg. She's Meg," Logan reminded.

Tia sat back without saying Meg's name the way her father was obviously prompting her to do.

"I wanna play wis you and An' Had," the little girl said quietly, pushing back on her pillow so she was more hidden by her father when she confided that to him.

"Aunt Had and I can't play tomorrow. Meg will be here for you to play with," he said with a pointed glance at Meg.

Why did he aim that at me? Meg wondered. Did he think she *wasn't* planning to play with his daughter?

Maybe she was misinterpreting the glance. Certainly she didn't address it. But she did lean forward so she could see Tia and say, "I have some games and you can show me what toys and games you have that you like to play."

"I wanna play wis my dad," Tia responded in a thanks-but-no-thanks way.

And why it flashed through Meg's mind that she might like to play with Tia's dad herself, Meg had no idea. But she nipped *that* bit of insanity in the bud, and said, "I'll tell you what, if you do what we need to do to get the day started, then as a prize, we'll go to a safe part of the workroom and visit your dad and your aunt Hadley for just a few minutes. Then, if you do whatever we need to do after that, you can get a second visit to see Dad and Aunt Hadley in the afternoon. As long as Dad says that's okay and that we won't disturb their work too much."

Tia looked up to her father for confirmation.

"I think that sounds like a good idea," he said. "But you'll have to do what Meg tells you to do first."

Meg was pleased that he'd gotten the idea—visiting him would be the reward earned for good behavior. She was also glad that he wasn't opposed to having his work disturbed.

Tia had also apparently gotten the idea that there was a price to be paid for the privilege, because she frowned mightily. But all she said to her father was, "Will you be here when I wake up?"

"I will be. We'll have breakfast together like we always do. Then I'll go out to the barn to work—like before, when we were at our old house, remember how I would leave to go to work?"

Tia nodded.

"Well, it's the same as that, except I don't go as far away. And while I do that, Meg will be with you like Nancy used to be."

At the mention of Nancy—who Meg could only

assume had been Tia's former nanny—Tia looked at Meg. "Hers like Nancy?" the little girl said, putting it together.

"Right. Nancy was your nanny in Connecticut, and now Meg is your nanny here—she'll help take care of you."

Tia seemed to accept Meg on those terms—luckily she must have had a good experience with Nancy.

But the acceptance came only in Tia not saying anything at all, but merely putting her index finger in her mouth. Which was apparently a signal to her father because seeing that, he got off the bed, slid the little girl to lie flat and covered her with her princess-themed top sheet and a light blanket.

Then he bent over, kissed Tia's forehead, and said, "Good night, moon. Good night, Tia."

Tia took her finger out of her mouth only long enough to say, "Guh'night, moon. Guh'night, Daddy."

And Meg had the sense that that was how they said good-night every night. It made her smile before she whispered, "See you tomorrow, Tia."

Out of the mouth came the index finger again. "Uh-uh. Say guh'night, moon. Guh'night, Tia."

"Ahh. Good night, moon. Good night, Tia," Meg said, following orders, thinking that it was a positive sign that she was being included in the ritual.

"Guh'night, moon. Guh'night, Meg," came the small, sleepy voice before the finger went back in the mouth once more and Tia closed her eyes.

Logan smoothed the little girl's hair lovingly and then nodded toward the door to let Meg know they should leave.

In the hallway outside Tia's room Logan pulled the door closed slightly and whispered, "We've been reading that same book and saying those same things every night for at least the last year but no one gets away without it."

"Bedtime routines are important for kids," Meg said. "They can almost be like a sleeping pill."

He nodded as if she wasn't telling him anything he didn't already know, and Meg wanted to kick herself for doing the second thing she'd vowed not to do with him—hide her introversion by saying everything as if it were a pearl of wisdom handed down from the mount of her education and experience.

But it was too late to do anything about it and so she just went with him downstairs.

Hadley was turning off the television in the living room when they got to the entry. Meg had left her luggage there before going up to watch Logan put Tia to bed but now there wasn't a suitcase in sight.

Before she could ask about it, Hadley said, "I took your things out to the apartment—I thought I'd save you guys that much."

"Thanks." This from Logan.

To Meg, Hadley said, "I think you'll love the apartment. I know I do. Logan put a lot of his own personal touches on it—and in it. He did everything but the plumbing and electrical work himself. He designed the cutest kitchen table, the couch and easy chairs are his, and the bed is one of his signature pieces, too."

"I can't wait to see it," Meg answered honestly, pretending not to notice how uncomfortable his sister's praise was making Logan.

"No reason to wait," he said then, as if he were in a hurry to get out of the situation. "Come on, I'll show it to you."

"I left the door unlocked," Hadley called as they headed for the rear of the house.

Still, Meg saw Logan grab a set of keys from one of the countertops as they passed through the dated but clean kitchen space. "These are yours," he told her, handing them to her. "There's a key to the apartment, keys to the front and back door of this house, and one that will get you into the barn. The only thing you don't have a key to is Chase's place, but I didn't think you'd ever need that," he explained.

"I know this place belonged to the Ludwigs before I left Northbridge," she said as Logan held the back door for her and she stepped into the warm summer evening air. "Did you buy the whole farm?"

"What was left of it to buy," Logan said, following her out. "Chase—Chase Mackey, I don't know if you knew or remember him…"

"The name is familiar but that's about it. He was your age, too, right? I was kind of oblivious to you all."

"Yeah, Chase is the same age as me. He's my business partner. And like a brother to me. Anyway, we bought the property that was left after most of it had been sold off in parts. I guess after old man Ludwig died his kids put the farm as a whole on the market. But when there were no buyers they started selling off parcels of land to the surrounding farms. The house, the garage, the barn and the four acres they sit on were harder to move. But they just happened to meet our needs—

personal and business—so Chase and I bought them," Logan explained as they crossed the backyard.

"I can tell the house has been freshly painted inside and out—"

"It didn't need much more work than that. But the garage and the barn are a different story," Logan said with a nod at the garage as they approached it. "The lower level of the garage will still be garage, but we added the apartment—that wasn't there at all originally. The barn will house our work- and showrooms, plus Chase and I have been putting a loft apartment in the upper half of that for him."

The garage and the barn were side by side behind the house—the barn directly behind it, the garage off to the left at the end of the driveway that veered around the farm-house. Not much distance separated any of it and they'd reached the garage where a whitewashed wooden staircase ran up one side to a private entrance to the apartment.

Logan motioned for Meg to go ahead of him. At the landing she opened the door and went in without waiting for him to do the honors. Hadley had left a table lamp on, so Meg's first glimpse of the place was well lit and as Logan came in after her, she said, "This is beautiful!"

And it was. Every detail from the oak cupboards to the chair rails to the hardwood floors to the one wall that was painted a rustic red shouted class and taste and at-tention to detail. It was so much more than a thrown-together garage apartment—which was what Meg had been afraid it might be.

"I'm glad you like it," Logan responded simply,

humbly, but in a way that made Meg think that he genuinely *was* glad he'd pleased her.

But she told herself she was probably reading more
into that than actually existed, and began to wander
around to look at everything close-up, thankful that she
wasn't going to be living somewhere awful and loving
the place so much she wanted to hug him.

Another unwarranted thought. And urge.

No playing with him, no hugging him, she warned
herself.

He showed her the bathroom and the closet, then
gave her a tour of the kitchen—reminding her that he
was hoping that rather than use it too much she would
be eating in the house with Tia, Hadley and himself.

"You could have just not put in a kitchen—that would
have made eating with you guys a necessity," she
pointed out.

"Not my style."

There was something sexy in the way he said that that
made her wonder what his style was.

But thinking of Logan McKendrick as sexy was
another item on Meg's List Of Don'ts. She instantly
added wondering what his style was to that same list.

"So, satisfy some curiosity for me, will you?" he
asked then, interrupting her internal struggle to keep her
mind on the straight and narrow.

"Sure," she agreed.

"With all your degrees and a big-deal job in Denver,
how is it that you're signing on to be Tia's nanny?"

It was a logical question that she'd been expecting. That
she had a ready answer for that didn't reveal too much.

"At Children's Hospital I see kids with all kinds of problems that are so much bigger than finding *Grilla* in the packing boxes or making sure everyone says good night, moon. I want to help them. I like helping them. But it's been a pretty steady dose of nothing but that for a while now and I just thought that I needed a little of the lighter side of kids for a change to recharge my battery."

He was watching her while she recited that. Studying her. And she could see in his handsome face that he wasn't completely buying it. But it was true. It just wasn't the whole story and she wasn't willing to tell him the rest. That would have to satisfy him.

And rather than saying any more, she countered with a question of her own.

"What about you? I don't know a lot about Mackey and McKendrick Furniture Designs but my sister, Kate, sends me the local newspaper and I did see an article— one of those Northbridge-boys-make-good things. I thought you'd built your business and your whole life in New York and Connecticut, but here you are."

He shrugged those broad shoulders. "It's a return to our roots," he said, giving her the sense that he was holding back, too. Quite a bit, if she were to make a guess.

But he hadn't pushed her so she didn't push him.

And as if they'd come to that by some kind of silent agreement, he nodded then, and said, "I'll leave and let you get started unpacking."

He headed for the door and Meg went with him, taking in the full and fabulous view of him from behind. His T-shirt outlined every muscle and his jeans molded a rear end that her hands inexplicably itched to cup.

"By the way," he said when he reached the door and was halfway across the threshold, turning around to look at her again. "If you want to bring Tia up here and spend tomorrow settling in, you can hold off a day or two before you get to her room. She's not really suffering the loss of Grilla, she's just peeved that she doesn't have him, so waiting a little longer isn't going to make any difference, and you might as well get comfortable before you dig into her stuff."

"That would be good. And are you really okay if I use visiting you while you work as a reward?"

"Sure. You'll see when you come out to the barn that the showroom is what you go into first—the workroom is behind it. Just holler to let me know you're there and I'll come out so Tia doesn't get near anything dangerous. But you can come anytime—feel free."

He made that sound like an invitation to her, not just as permission to bring Tia. But that probably wasn't what he'd intended. They were just two people with one aim—to care for his daughter—and Meg told herself that she needed to stop reading too much into things. The same way she needed to stop noticing every little detail about him and finding something sexy in them all.

She didn't understand what was going on with her. It wasn't something she'd ever done before with anyone else. And if ever there was a wrong time, place, situation or person, this was it!

So she did a mental pulling-in-on-the-reins, again hoping that her reaction to him had something to do with novelty and that when she got to know Logan better she'd be able to take him more in stride.

"I appreciate the open-door policy, but I won't abuse it. I have a lot of tricks up my sleeves when it comes to getting children to behave and comply—rewarding Tia with a visit to you will only be one of them," she told him, hearing the formality that had crept into her tone but unable to stop it because it was just something she was accustomed to hiding behind the way Tia had hidden behind Logan tonight.

He must have caught the slight alteration of tone, though, because his eyebrows beetled together slightly. But he didn't say anything about it.

Instead he merely went on. "Tia isn't one of those crack-of-dawn kids—she'll usually sleep until eight or nine, so you can take your time coming over in the morning. Unless you're an early riser and you need coffee—there will be a pot brewed long before Tia is up and you're welcome to it."

Meg imagined going over at sunrise to start her day with him alone, in the quiet of the morning, just the two of them...

Much, much too appealing a thought!

"Let's just see how it goes," she said noncommittally, hating how more of that aloofness had echoed in her voice.

"Sure. Whatever," Logan said, those furrows in his brow deepening.

Then he said good-night and left, and once again Meg wanted to kick herself.

One minute she'd been friendly, the next she'd been evasive, the next she'd talked like a textbook—if he was worried that he'd hired some kind of nut job he had good reason.

She was just so all over the place when it came to him.

But tomorrow was another day, she consoled herself. It was her first day of work, when her complete focus would be on Tia.

That would probably help, she told herself.

No, not *probably*, that would *have* to help.

Because she'd come here to get herself back on track.

Not to hook up with a hot hunk.

Chapter Three

"Oh-oh, look-ut Harry did...."

At the sound of Tia's voice, Meg stopped putting clothes in a dresser drawer and glanced around to find that the puppy had gone into the apartment's bathroom, grabbed the end of the toilet paper and unrolled it all the way out into the living room.

"Harry, not again!" Meg complained because it was the third time the puppy had done that.

Despite the repeat performance, Tia thought it was hilarious. And as much of a nuisance as the mess was, the fact that it delighted the three-year-old made it worth it to Meg. That kind of simple joy was part of why she was there—it was actually part of what she was hoping to find in this job that was her self-prescribed therapy.

Tia knew the drill by then—she grabbed Harry to

keep him from running wild and unrolling even more of the paper while Meg tore off what he'd slobbered on, threw it away, and re-rolled the rest. By the time she'd done that and come out of the bathroom—again leaving the door open to accommodate Tia's instant dashes there when she decided at the last minute that she needed to use the facilities—a giggling Tia was sitting on the floor with Max licking her face.

Meg could have left the puppies at the house while she and Tia were at the garage apartment unpacking. But where Tia went, the puppies wanted to go, too, and Meg hadn't had the heart to separate them. Still, it had made settling in a slow process and by late Monday afternoon—after spending the entire day trying to empty her suitcases and the boxes she'd taken from the trunk of her car—she was still only about half finished.

"Are we done yet?" Tia asked when Max and Harry began to wrestle with each other and ignore her.

"Just a little while longer and then it will be time to go back to the house to get ready for dinner. I have a present for you, though, since you've been so good today and let me get some of my work done."

"A present?" Tia repeated.

She sounded wide-eyed but Meg couldn't actually see the little girl's eyes because they were covered with a pair of old sunglasses Meg had let her have. They completed the dress-up ensemble that included one of Meg's scarves and two of her belts wrapped around Tia's T-shirt and shorts, and a pair of Meg's thong panties worn like a backpack with Tia's shoulders through the leg openings. Meg had no idea what Tia thought the panties were, but since the three-year-old had devised her own use for them and not asked about their real purpose, Meg had not offered the information.

"What kind of present?" Tia asked coyly.

This particular present was one of Meg's favorite tools and she was surprised that Tia had been distracted and entertained with other things for so long that it had taken until now for Meg to need to bring it out. Ordinarily, with the kids she worked with, she needed to use the tools at her disposal immediately.

She was also thrilled that it hadn't taken more than today for Tia to become comfortable with her—she was accustomed to kids who were so disabled, fearful, phobic, angry, upset or just plain leery of strangers that it took far longer to win them over.

"It's kind of a big present," Meg answered her charge's question in a tone intended to intrigue.

"How big?" Tia inquired, going for the bait.

"Pretty big," Meg said as she went to the bed. She'd hidden the gift under it when she'd taken it out of her trunk last night after having brought her car around to park it nearer to the apartment—something Hadley had come across the yard to suggest after Logan had left, making Meg wonder why he hadn't come back himself.

Not that it mattered...

"It's too big a present to wrap," she warned Tia as she got down on her knees and pulled out the mini trampoline.

"What is it?" Tia asked when she saw it.

Meg positioned it next to the bed so the mattress could act as a sort of guardrail. "It's called a trampoline."

"What d'ya do with it?"

Meg stepped onto it and demonstrated. "You jump on it."

This time Tia's awe was more apparent because her mouth opened wide.

"Le'me do it!" Tia demanded, jumping up and down on the floor in an excited mimicry of Meg's demonstration on the trampoline. And again Meg appreciated the fact that it was so easy to interest Tia, to excite her, and that she was so willing to plunge right into even new things.

Meg stepped off the trampoline and before she could offer any assistance, Tia had climbed onto it.

"First let's get some of this stuff off of you—you could trip on the ends of the belts and the scarf, and the sunglasses will go flying," she explained.

"But not my pitty cape," Tia said, patting one of the thong's straps at her shoulder.

"Not your pretty cape," Meg agreed. "You can keep that on as long as we're up here but it will have to stay in the apartment when we leave." Because there was no way she was taking Tia to dinner wearing her flowered thong…

While Meg divested Tia of the rest of her playthings, the little girl could hardly contain herself. When she'd finished, Meg said, "Now hold my hands and take little jumps at first, until you get the feel of it."

Tia didn't hesitate to do as she'd been told—anything to finally get to do what she was wiggling around in eager anticipation of. But the exact moment her tiny hands were securely in Meg's, Tia jumped. Tentatively at first, giggling, then jumping more.

"I yike it!" she proclaimed, venturing a higher jump, wobbling slightly on the landing but not enough to fall.

Then she got braver still and began to jump repeatedly. Up and down, up and down—she was clearly a quick learner, and after a few minutes of that said, "Le'me do it myself."

By then Meg thought Tia knew what she was doing and since the trampoline was barely a foot off the floor with nothing nearby that the little girl could fall into and hurt herself, Meg allowed her to let go of her hands.

"Now go back," Tia ordered, her three-year-old independence making her insist that Meg not continue to hover.

But Meg only went as far as to sit on the bed. She still wanted to keep an eye on the little girl until she was sure Tia could manage the trampoline without incident, but she was also enjoying watching how much pleasure it was bringing the happy-go-lucky Tia. That was more important to her than unpacking.

This was exactly why she'd taken the nanny job—to have contact again with an untroubled, carefree kid. A kid who experienced unfettered joy over things like the dog unraveling toilet paper, who had no compunctions about innocently wearing a thong as a makeshift cape, who got a thrill out of jumping on a tiny trampoline.

Things like that were what had made Meg enjoy working with kids in the first place. Prior to taking on the job of dealing with the serious aspects of ill, disabled or abused children, being with kids had just been fun. It had been a way for her to get out of the shell of her shy, reserved nature and behave more freely herself.

And that had been important to her. Especially since

she worried that her shy, reserved nature made her a little too much like her grandfather, the stuffy former town reverend.

Not that she was in any way as judgmental or staunch or strident or daunting as the Reverend was. But she did tend toward being a bit on the controlled side, and she'd discovered early on that working with kids helped counteract that. And right now she needed that more than she ever had.

In fact, if she didn't find a way to accomplish it, she wasn't sure that she could go on doing her job as a psychologist anymore.

Intellectually, she knew what she was going through—it was a reaction to a traumatic event. But she was concerned that if she didn't do something to work through it in a hurry, her inhibited, reticent, shy nature might take over and she might not ever lose the jitters or the skittishness she'd developed. The jitters and the skittishness that made her jump at even the smallest unexpected sound or every time one of her kids came near her without warning. She was worried this fearfulness might make her as suspicious and untrusting as her grandfather was, that she would end up distant and off-putting and untouchable.

Why did the image of Logan McKendrick pop into her mind when she thought about how much she didn't want to be untouchable?

It wasn't as if she was there to be touched by the man who was her boss. Or by any other man, for that matter.

She had things to sort out. Things that had put her at a critical juncture in her life, in her career. There was no way she needed the additional complication of romance with anyone, let alone someone who was employing her to take care of his daughter.

And his daughter was another component of that. Tia could potentially be hurt by something like her nanny having a fling with her father. It was one thing for the McKendricks to include Meg and *treat* her like family, but it was another thing to play house and give Tia a false sense of a family that didn't really exist.

And yet the thought that she wouldn't want Logan to see her as untouchable lingered the same way his image and the strong sense of him had stayed with her since he'd left last night…

Maybe that lingering image and sense of him came from the fact that there was so much of him in this apartment. A sort of essence of him left in his handiwork and in the personal touches that almost seemed like a brand on the place. He'd built it, for crying out loud. And not only had he furnished it, he'd furnished it with pieces he'd designed, pieces he'd created himself.

Just then Tia jumped too near the springs and lost her balance for a split second before she regained it and went on the way she had been.

It seemed to Meg that that was what she was going through herself—she'd lost her balance and now she was back in Northbridge, working with Tia, to regain her own equilibrium.

And regardless of how terrific-looking Logan was, how sexy, how appealing he could be when he was holding his daughter on his lap or reading to her or gently kissing her good-night and tucking her in, appreciating him as a good dad was as far as anything was going to go with him.

Because nothing could be more unbalancing than a relationship with a man and that was the last thing she needed right now.

"I'll walk out with you."

"Okay," Meg agreed much too easily when Logan made that suggestion late Monday evening.

After the family dinner, giving Tia her bath while Logan answered a business call, and sitting in again on the reading of *Goodnight Moon* before putting Tia to bed, it had amounted to almost a fourteen-hour workday for Meg. She should have been ready for some time to herself.

Instead, having Logan come with her out the back door gave her a whole new surge of energy.

"So how was your first full day on the job? Are you ready to run for the hills yet?" he asked as they strolled across the yard.

"Not yet," she answered with a laugh that didn't give away how much she'd liked every minute she'd spent alone with Tia, and then every minute on top of that that had included him.

"I wanted to talk to you about tomorrow," he said then. "After Tia's nap Hadley and Tia and I are supposed to go meet Theresa Grayson—I don't know if you know what's going on with that…"

Since her sister, Kate, was marrying Ry Grayson— Theresa's grandson—on Friday night and Meg was the maid of honor, she actually did know what Logan was alluding to.

And she didn't see any reason to play dumb, so she said, "I do know about Theresa Grayson. I know that fifty-plus years ago when she was seventeen, her parents were killed and she was taken in by Hector Tyson and his wife. That Hector—who is Northbridge's cocurmudgeon along with my grandfather—seduced her and got her pregnant and then arranged for the baby to be secretly adopted. I know that Theresa has a lot of mental and emotional problems and came back here desperate to reconnect with the daughter she'd given up, that her grandkids have been working diligently to do that for her—"

"And that they found out that Theresa's child was actually Hadley's and my mother," Logan interjected.

"Which makes Theresa Grayson your grandmother," Meg concluded.

"And tomorrow is the first time we come face-to-face."

They'd reached the steps that ran alongside the garage up to the apartment, but Logan didn't seem inclined to go the rest of the way because he leaned his T-shirted back against the garage's outer wall, hooked his thumbs into his jeans pockets and raised a booted foot to the bottom step.

It was a lovely summer's night and Meg didn't mind standing outside talking to him so she stopped there, too, facing him and resting her own back against the stair rail.

But even if it had been twenty degrees below zero she wouldn't have been in any hurry to say good-night.

"Are you nervous about meeting Theresa?" she asked, part of her attention on what they were talking about and another part of it looking at the play of light and shadow on the sharply drawn lines of his features.

"It's a strange position to be in, but no, I'm not nervous about it. Except maybe when it comes to Tia," he said. "Hadley and I have been warned that things with Theresa could go in a lot of different directions—she could refuse to see us at the last minute or cry all the way through it or be disoriented or just quiet. We don't know what to expect."

"Kate introduced me to her and I know Theresa's diagnosis. Multiple diagnoses, actually. Yes, she has a lot of problems, but you won't find a raving crazy woman—if that's what you're afraid of. I'd say that if she can get up the courage to actually meet you and Hadley, the worst you'll see is tears because she's very emotional. But she also may just be happy to meet you and not appear any different than anyone else."

"I'm actually less worried about her than I am about Tia," Logan confided.

His pale eyes were iridescent in the light cast from the four lamps that were hung at the same angle that the stairs ran along the garage wall. And even in the dimness Meg thought those eyes exuded a warmth she could almost feel. Except that she told herself she was probably only imagining that...

"Tia could love Theresa or hate her on sight," he was saying when Meg forced her focus back to that. "And she could behave or misbehave accordingly. I don't want her to set off someone who—from what I've heard—is pretty easily upset. I'd like it if you could just come with us so if Tia acts up, you can take her outside."

"Sure, absolutely," she said, agreeing enthusiastically—and resisting the urge to spout technical terminology. "Certainly Tia doesn't need a psychologist there, you just need someone who can remove her if she puts up a fuss like any three-year-old might around new people in a strange situation."

"Exactly," Logan confirmed.

"You said this is the first time you'll be meeting Theresa, but what about her other grandchildren? That would make Wyatt, Marti and Ry your new cousins— have you met them yet?"

"Yeah, the triplets," he answered. "They all came out last week to fill us in on things," Logan continued. "It was a pretty big shock to Hadley and me to find out that we're related. That our mom had been adopted."

"You had no idea?" Meg asked.

"Not a clue. Neither did our mother, apparently. We've talked to our other grandmother—Mom's adopted mother—"

"My sister, Kate, told me it was Anne and Shamus Wimmer who adopted the baby."

"Right. Gramps passed away a few years ago, but Gran is still alive and lives in Florida. When we first found out about this whole thing we called her. It took some persuading but she finally told us the truth. They never let anyone know they'd adopted. Apparently Gran even pretended to be pregnant at the same time Theresa was and then made a birth announcement as if she'd had the baby. And they never told a single soul anything different, including the rest of their families and my mother."

"Who passed away, too, if I'm remembering right."

"When Hadley was almost three and I was five. She was pregnant with what would have been our baby brother and there were complications. They both died," Logan confirmed. "But Mom died never knowing anything about being adopted."

"Or suspecting anything?"

"I'm sure she didn't. To my grandparents, she was a gift—they doted on her and adored her. Which is more than I can say for Hadley and I being raised by a stepmother. But then I guess adopted kids are more wanted than stepkids."

"That was what you and Hadley ended up as—stepkids…" Meg said to prompt him to go on. Because not only did she want to have her facts straight, but since he'd added that, it was obviously on his mind and she thought he might want to talk about it.

She must have been right because he didn't hesitate to go on.

"My father remarried six months later—Hadley was two and a half, I had just turned five. He said kids needed a mother and he couldn't take care of us on his own. And almost nine months to the day after that wedding the second batch of McKendricks started to arrive—the *real* family, according to my stepmother," Logan said with an edge of bitterness to his tone. "She never let anyone forget that Hadley and I weren't her kids, and she didn't hide her resentment that she'd been stuck raising another woman's children."

"That's awful," Meg said simply.

After a moment, Logan collected himself, smiling a half smile and said, "What were we talking about that got us onto this?"

But looking at the curve of his mouth when it formed

that smile stalled Meg's memory and made her think something else.

It made her think about kissing him.

The thoughts were out of the blue, uninvited and unwelcome, but there they were anyway—she was wondering what it might be like for him to kiss her. Wondering and wanting him to—just a little…

Meg forced herself to veer away from that, to actually answer his question. "I believe we were talking about me going with you guys tomorrow when you meet Theresa so I can wrangle Tia if need be," she finally said, relieved that she'd been able to pull it together enough to make the recollection.

"Ah, that's right. So, you don't mind?"

"I'm happy to," she assured.

"Can I ask you one more thing?"

"Sure."

"Tia said she wore a cape of yours today and she wants one of her own…"

The thong panties.

Meg hadn't heard Tia say that but just knowing what the little girl was referring to made her cheeks heat. She hoped it wasn't visible in the porch light. She also had no idea how she was going to explain the *cape* without abject embarrassment.

Lie. That was all she could think to do.

"It was just a towel I tied around her shoulders. I'm sure she'll forget all about it by tomorrow." At least Meg hoped to high heaven that she did…

She hoped, too, that the faint frown that tugged at Logan's brows again didn't mean that Tia had described her *cape* in enough detail for him to know it couldn't have been merely a towel.

But rather than give him the opportunity to question her more about it, she took the first two steps toward her apartment to indicate that it was time for this to end.

Logan apparently got the hint because he said, "I should let you get going." He pushed off the garage wall to stand up straight.

Between her raised height on the steps and his movement forward, for a moment they were so near that her breasts were just a whisper from meeting his chest. So near that it would have taken next to nothing for him to kiss her just the way she was sort of wishing he would...

He pivoted in a hurry, though, and that ended that.

"See you in the morning," Logan said then, as if nothing had happened. Because with the exception of invading each other's space a little, nothing had.

"See you in the morning," Meg repeated, her voice quiet.

But as she began to climb the remaining stairs, she knew she was going to be seeing him much, much sooner than the next morning. She was actually still seeing him as she went into her apartment. Seeing him in her mind's eye.

And even though it was something that had been happening over and over again since she'd met the man, this was a new, more vivid, more real image of him. An image that not only included how great-looking he was, but how fabulous he smelled, and how powerful a presence that muscular body was up close, and how he seemed to give off a kind of heat that had made her melt a little inside...

An image that she knew was also now going to include how much taller he was when they were nearly chest-to-chest, and how much he would have to bend, how much she would have to rise, in order for their mouths to meet...

I'm supposed to be fighting these kinds of thoughts, she reminded herself as she closed the door behind her.

And there in the dark of the studio apartment that Logan had built, fight them she did.

Only they were stronger than she was...

Chapter Four

Meg thought that the meeting with Theresa Grayson on Tuesday afternoon couldn't have gone better. Despite voicing some pre-meeting jitters, Logan and Hadley had obviously relaxed within minutes of going into the Graysons' house. More than just behaving well, having Tia there had served to cut some of the older woman's tension, awkwardness and emotion. Tia had provided an upbeat and unifying focus for everyone, including Marti, Wyatt, Ry, the nurse-caregiver Mary Pat, and Meg.

The explanation of who Theresa was had gone over Tia's head but she'd accepted the suggestion that she call her Great-Gram. And after some initial shyness, Tia had even agreed to sit on Great-Gram's lap. Only briefly, but Theresa had seemed pleased.

Tia had been thrilled with having cookies served on

china and juice in a cup and saucer. She had liked that there were flowers on the dinnerware. The little girl's only faux pas was to turn her nose up at the small, beautifully handcarved wooden sleigh that Theresa had given her—one of Theresa's own childhood toys. Tia had politely asked what it did and showed her disinterest by setting it aside after she learned that it didn't actually *do* anything.

Logan, on the other hand, had admired it and Meg suspected it would end up belonging to him.

Meg had also been glad to see how open, friendly and welcoming Marti, Wyatt and Ry were to Logan and Hadley. The three grandchildren who had guardianship of Theresa and who had spent their lives sharing her care showed no qualms at all about having two more family members introduced into the mix. Instead, they'd seemed open to including Logan and Hadley, and making them as much a part of Theresa's life as Logan and Hadley wanted to be, giving them an open invitation to visit anytime.

For Logan's and Hadley's part, Meg had not been able to tell much about what they were thinking or feeling beyond a continuing shock to have so recently found out that their background wasn't what they'd always believed it to be. But there hadn't been time to talk about any of it because when they'd all arrived home again they discovered an overflowing toilet had wreaked some havoc in the downstairs bathroom.

While Logan found the water shutoff and Hadley tried to do some cleanup, Meg had taken Tia with her to the apartment where Tia couldn't get into the mess that the three-year-old saw as a chance for indoor-puddle-jumping.

From the apartment, Meg called her brother Noah. Noah was the local contractor and he promised to get his plumber there right away.

Dinner ended up being sandwiches that Meg made, leaving a plate of them for Logan, Hadley and the plumber, and taking hers and Tia's outdoors for an impromptu picnic. Then she'd given Tia her bath at the apartment and when the plumbing problems were fixed, Hadley had come to get Tia to take her home to bed, ending a day that was in no way lacking activity.

What it had lacked—for Meg—was any kind of concentrated time with Logan. Which shouldn't have been an issue. And yet it had her feeling restless and deprived just when she should have been relaxing.

It was ridiculous, she told herself again and again as she finished what was left of her unpacking. Logan was nothing more than a peripheral part of why she was there, and seeing him only in conjunction with the events of the day—the same way she'd seen Hadley— shouldn't have made a single bit of difference.

And yet it wasn't Hadley she kept thinking about.

It was Logan…

By ten o'clock the overhead lights and the table lamps had been on all evening, causing the apartment to be hot and stuffy. Between that and the absurdly low spirits Meg had been left in because Logan hadn't been a part of her evening, she decided to open all the windows, turn off the lights, and sit outside until the place cooled off. And maybe she would, too…

It didn't help much that when she went to sit on the stair landing she was facing the rear of the main house and looking right into the window over the kitchen sink. Or that she could see Logan there.

He was looking downward, washing his hands, his angular face expressionless, the lower half of it stubbled by a five-o'clock shadow that gave him a sexy, scruffy, bad-boy air.

He'd taken off the shirt he'd been wearing to meet his newest grandmother and now had on only a white crewneck T-shirt that fitted him like a second skin and left no doubt about how well built his upper body was—including the massive biceps that stretched the short sleeves tight.

Did he still have on the jeans he'd been wearing earlier? Meg wondered. Or was he ready for bed and in pajama pants? Or did he wear pajamas at all? Maybe he was just in his shorts…

Ashamed of herself for even thinking that, Meg clamped her eyes shut and shook her head.

But a moment later, when she heard the main house's back door creak, she opened her eyes just in time to see Logan step out onto the deck.

The jeans. He was still wearing the jeans—just tight enough to accentuate that remarkable lower half, not so tight that they looked like he had anything to prove.

And she didn't know if he'd caught sight of her from the kitchen window when she'd had her eyes closed, or just as he'd come outside, but he gave her a little wave and headed across the yard.

That was enough to speed up her pulse even if he hadn't had such a great walk. But he really did have a great walk.

It wasn't something she'd ever noticed with anyone else, but drinking in the sight of every step he took with the faintest bit of swagger, sent her pulse into full double time.

She half expected him to stay standing at the bottom of the stairs but he didn't. And as he climbed them, Meg moved over to make room for him.

He didn't come all the way to the landing to sit, though. He sat on the step below her, turned toward her, and braced himself on an elbow on the landing so he was facing her almost as if he were lying down.

Meg pivoted to face him, too, having a slight advantage over him that let her look straight at him without much distance separating them and with the full glow of the outside lights bathing those striking features. And she couldn't keep from smiling for no reason other than that she was just so unreasonably pleased she was getting a few minutes alone with him after all...

It was the weary sigh that came with his settling in that prompted her to say, "Plumbing problems fixed?"

"Finally. You know that last trip to the bathroom that I sent Tia on just before we left? Well, it got Diving Man flushed," Logan said.

Diving Man was Tia's tub toy.

"Ah, she was complaining when I gave her tonight's bath over here that she didn't have Diving Man."

"She won't ever have him again—Diving Man tried to make a run for it all the way out to the pipes and got stuck. We had to pull the whole toilet off and break him in half to get him out. Which made Tia mad."

While Meg knew that Logan was tired and had just had

to tear his bathroom apart as a result of the three-year-old, Meg was having trouble suppressing a laugh.

Which Logan must have been able to tell because he cracked a tight-lipped smile himself even as he chastised, "It wasn't funny."

"I don't know, if you're Diving Man the tub is pretty much just snorkeling, but the toilet is the real deal— deep-sea scuba diving, isn't it? Tia was just giving him the bigger adventure," she said as laughter took over.

"Yeah, I suppose," Logan agreed, giving in to laughter himself. "That kid's gonna give me gray hair."

But it was such nice hair—thick and just unruly enough to add to his sex appeal. Brown or gray, it would still be fabulous hair…

Of course that wasn't what Meg said. She said, "So from now on tub toys stay out of Tia's reach until she's in the tub to play with them and has supervision?"

"And let's remind her a lot about what *doesn't* get flushed," Logan added as if they were a team.

"Poor Diving Man—you ruined all his fun," Meg teased, making Logan laugh again.

"What a day," he said then.

"I'll say," she agreed to commiserate with him. "Diver-recovery on top of meeting a grandmother you didn't know you had and becoming part of a whole other family."

"Yeah, that was weird, wasn't it—meeting Theresa and having perfect strangers talking about Hadley and Tia and me being their family?"

"I understand *that* weirdness completely," Meg commiserated.

"Because you sort of had the same thing happen, didn't you?"

"We did end up meeting one of our grandmothers— Celeste—only recently," she confirmed, unsure how much of her own situation Logan knew about since he'd been out of Northbridge during the discoveries and revelations that had recently changed the dynamics of her own family.

"I know the Reverend's wife running off with bank robbers was one of the old town scandals," he said.

"Not to mention that it was the Reverend's biggest embarrassment. But before you or I were even born, she slipped back into town, calling herself Leslie—"

"The large lady who worked at the dry cleaners."

"Right. It was all the weight she'd gained after she ran away and then was deserted by her lover that made her unrecognizable. When she realized that, she reinvented herself and became just another Northbridge newcomer."

"Nobody figured it out until now?"

"The Reverend figured out who she was but only after a few years and a slip of the tongue she made that gave her away. But even then he didn't tell anyone because he liked that she had to stay on the sidelines of her own family—it was his retribution. But all that time she was right here—our grandmother and we didn't even know it. Now that we do, we've all been working at a relationship with her in our own ways."

"In other words, most families have some weirdness to them?" Logan said.

"I don't think there's a lot of families with weirdnesses quite like yours or mine, but to some extent families can frequently have some twisted history to them that people have to deal with."

"So how are you working at a relationship with Celeste-who-was-Leslie?" Logan asked.

"I can't say I've done a whole lot," she admitted confidentially.

"But you *are* making an effort?"

"Sure. She's family…"

"And you think I should make an effort with Theresa?"

"I'd never tell you what to do or not to do with that, no," Meg was quick to say.

"But in your own situation, regardless of the history, Celeste is family and you're treating her accordingly."

"That's just me. It isn't a model for what anyone else should do."

He smiled again, this time knowingly. "Family is important to you even if part of that family includes someone who ran off with a bank robber and the Reverend—who couldn't have been a lot of laughs to have as a grandfather."

"No laughs at all," Meg confirmed.

"What kind of an impact did the Reverend have on you?"

It was Meg's turn to smile knowingly. "You've been wondering that since you remembered he's my grandfather when we first talked on Saturday. And making assumptions about it," Meg said, wishing it hadn't come out quite as coyly as it had.

"Have I?" he challenged with another half smile of his own and a hint of flirting to his tone, too.

"The whole communal-living thing," Meg said. "I

saw the wheels turning in your head when I wanted to make sure I hadn't misunderstood the living arrangements. You remembered who my grandfather is and thought I was a huge prude."

His grin gave him away and let her know that was exactly what he'd thought. "A little prudishness in a nanny is probably a good thing. I just liked giving you a hard time. But *did* being the Reverend's granddaughter make you a *huge* prude?"

"I wouldn't say *huge*—"

"That *is* what you said."

"I said that was what you thought I was," she persisted.

"Okay, so maybe you're not a *huge* prude, but you are a prude?"

She knew he was enjoying giving her a hard time. But she didn't mind. She was enjoying their back-and-forth just as much. Probably more than she should have been.

"I'd say that there's a little of the prude in me, yes," she conceded reluctantly.

"Uh-huh…" he said as if that were a given. "And what else did being the Reverend's granddaughter make you?"

"Oh, I don't know…Worried about being offensive if I'm too bold or outspoken, I guess. According to my grandfather a female's place is only in the background, in a serving position, hoping a man—any man—will want her and make her worth something."

"He doesn't think girls are worth anything otherwise?"

"No. It's part of a girls-aren't-as-good-as-boys mentality that also made me feel as if I had to be twice as diligent and work harder than everyone else just to matter. And I suppose I'll always have a second-class citizen sort of insecurity and self-image—"

"Second-class citizen? That's so wrong…"

"I agree with you. But when you grow up under someone who tells you how unworthy you are over and over again, it has an effect."

"A rotten one."

She liked that he was so outraged by the stance that she'd hated all her life, too. "I said that all members of a family have an impact, I didn't say it was always a good one. But it did make me ambitious—more quietly than most people, but still, that pushed me to get my education and to do what I've done so far."

"I'll bet there were some strict limitations on dating."

"You'd win that bet! Anything other than going out with a group of kids was prohibited until senior prom—and we all had a strict eleven-o'clock curfew even that night."

"You're kidding!"

"Nope. Not that we didn't all date under the cloak of going out with a group, but until senior prom we had to use that cover. And then worry that we'd be found out—it put a crimp in things. For me, at least, not a lot of boys wanted to bother with the subterfuge."

Logan shook his head. "I don't know what was wrong with those boys!"

Meg appreciated his compliment and laughed. "Then, too, I was painfully bashful and awkward and tongue-tied around boys, so even if the Reverend's rules hadn't been in place, I doubt there would have been a line of guys waiting outside my door."

"So you were a late-bloomer." He said that as if there was no question that she'd blossomed.

It was flattering for Meg who had trouble seeing herself that way. It was especially flattering when he was looking at her as if he did. And, like the previous night, she blushed. Only tonight it didn't have anything to do with embarrassment over Tia calling the thong panties a cape. It had to do with the warmth that seemed to be coming from Logan. From eyes that just might have held the kind of appreciation and attraction she felt every time she looked at him.

But then he took a deep breath and sighed. "I suppose I should let you get to bed. Tomorrow will be here before we know it and it's anybody's guess what Tia will be up to."

"I'm taking her to a playgroup in the Town Square, if that's all right," Meg said, willing him not to go. Not just yet...

"Yeah, she told me. I was tempted to punish her for the Diving Man incident by telling her she couldn't go but I couldn't do it," he admitted.

"That would have been kind of a big gun to bring out for a small infraction. Plus getting to play with other kids is really important for her." Meg was doing her best not to slip into lecture-mode again. And as she gazed at Logan so nearby, as she looked into those eyes that turned silvery in that light, at that face she just wanted to trace with her fingertips, all she could really think about was kissing...

"So you're telling me that it's good that I didn't punish her by taking away something she needs—like food or water or air or getting to know the kids she has to make friends with to be happy here?" Logan said with a smile that announced that she was once again telling him something he already knew.

"That's what I'm telling you," she said, making it obvious that she was merely playing along.

Apparently he liked that because he grinned at her once again.

But that grin drew her attention to his supple mouth and just made her think about kissing all the more…

And it didn't help that he still wasn't looking at her the way any boss before him ever had. He was looking at her the way men she'd been on successful dates with had. Men she'd ended up having relationships with.

Close, personal, *kissing* relationships…

And she was suddenly very aware of their positions again. Of how little distance separated them. Of her own advantage.

She would only have to lean forward a few inches and she could kiss him…

Wouldn't *that* surprise him! He'd never expect the Reverend's granddaughter to do that!

And she wanted to. So much it shocked her. So much she felt herself actually move in. Barely. But some…

Did he move, too? Upward? Toward her?

If he did it was so scant she couldn't be sure. But he might have…

Did that mean it would be all right for her to kiss him? That he might even want her to?

She wanted to.

She really, really wanted to…

But she couldn't just up and kiss the man, she told herself. Not a man who she wasn't convinced beyond the shadow of a doubt wanted her to kiss him. Not a man who hadn't kissed her first.

But she *had* leaned in a little and she suddenly felt the need to make it seem like that had been for another reason. So she added to it and used it as the arch that swept her up to her feet as if she were just taking seriously his suggestion that they say good-night.

Logan didn't immediately follow suit. He stayed lounging there on her steps. And he let his eyes take a long, slow rise right up the length of her until they met hers.

Then he smiled, knowingly again, and she didn't think for a minute that she'd fooled him.

But he didn't say anything. He just pushed off the landing with his elbow and got to his feet, too, taking a few steps down before he even glanced at her again.

"Thanks for making the sandwiches and keeping Tia out of the way tonight," he said over his shoulder as he sauntered down the remaining stairs, giving no indication that anything might have passed between them.

"Sure," Meg said in a voice more soft than she wanted it to be.

"See you in the morning."

"See you in the morning," she repeated.

Then she watched him cross back to the house with that sexy-as-hell walk that was even better going than it had been coming.

And she just couldn't help wondering what it might have been like if she *had* had the courage to kiss him.

If he would have balked.

Or would he have taken what she'd started and run with it…

He probably would have balked because it would have been so out of line, she told herself firmly.

But deep down?

She thought there was just the faintest chance that he might have grabbed her by the arms, pulled her close, taken what she'd started and made it into something even better.

And it was that image that followed her right inside her apartment and all the way through the rest of the night…

Chapter Five

"How did Tia do at the playgroup in Town Square today?" Logan asked on Wednesday evening.

Meg was sitting with him in the outdoor bleachers of the high-school field at a baseball game being played by the local sports team that called themselves the Bruisers. They were a group of Northbridge men who got together to play whatever sport was in season, dividing into two groups to compete against each other. It was a casual thing that had become a year-round, weekly event that most of the town turned out to watch.

When Logan had suggested to Meg that they go, her first impression had been that he was asking her on a date.

In anticipation of that, while Tia napped at the apartment after playgroup, Meg had showered a second time, shampooed her hair, pressed one of her favorite blouses—

a white eyelet she wore over a tanktop—and chosen a new pair of Capri slacks that made her ankles look thin.

Then, at dinner, she'd discovered that Hadley and Tia were also going.

Which, of course, made more sense and prompted Meg to remind herself that she needed to keep her dealings with Logan on a professional level regardless of how relaxed things were.

It was now after eight and Hadley had just opted to take Tia home to put her to bed, leaving Meg and Logan alone after all. Still, Meg steadfastly refused to entertain the idea that this was anything more than it was. Even if Logan suddenly seemed more interested in talking than in watching the game.

Meg answered his question about the playgroup. "Tia did about what I expected her to do. She was shy and just wanted to stay with me at first. Then she wanted to play, but she wanted me to go with her. But eventually the appeal of the slide and the shovels and dump trucks in the sandbox was stronger than she was."

Something Meg understood because she kept having the same experience with Logan—his appeal repeatedly became stronger than her resolve to resist it…

But she chased that thought away and went on with what she'd been saying.

"Eventually Tia did leave my side, but she didn't go far and she made sure she could see me and that I was within hearing range—that's a normal attachment response."

Instant frown. Meg knew *attachment response* had brought it on. But on top of combating the earlier illusion that this was a date, she was also dealing with the memory of how close she'd come to kissing Logan the night before. And if nothing else, the ability to be the authority on the subject of a three-year-old's development gave her the feeling that she had at least a little control.

Otherwise, she was just the ditz who couldn't stop noticing even the smallest details about this man. The ditz who had almost made the supreme mistake of kissing her boss last night. The ditz who had thought she was being asked on a date when she wasn't…

"Did Tia join in with the other kids at all?" Logan asked without commenting on Meg's formal-sounding assessment.

"Yes, Tia did very well. She didn't show any signs of aggressive behavior. When she wanted a toy someone else had, she either waited for them to leave it behind or she came and asked me to make them give it to her—"

"Oh-oh, have I spoiled her so much she thinks she can have anything she wants, even if it belongs to another kid?"

Meg shook her head. "The toys were all there for everyone to play with, they didn't *belong* to any one child. And it's normal for a three-year-old to think she should have anything she wants. What Tia was doing was trying to find a way to get what she wanted without making it a battle—she wanted me to be her problem-solver. And when I explained to her that she had to wait her turn, she accepted that."

"Okay…" he said as if he wasn't sure why Meg hadn't merely said that in the first place. "So she got along with the other kids?"

"She did. And she made some connections—you heard her at dinner—she remembers the names of the other children, she knew which ones she liked and which ones she didn't like—"

"She didn't like the boy in the red shirt who picked his nose and the mean girl who hit Howie—whoever Howie is."

So he listened when his daughter talked, too. Meg was glad to know that.

"Right—she didn't like the nose-picker and the hitter," Meg confirmed. "She was protective of Howie and stood up to the bully who wanted Howie's shovel, and when Howie was afraid of going down the slide Tia suggested they go down together."

"Yeah, I thought she must have liked Howie when his name kept coming up. And there was someone else…Bet'ny?" Logan said the name he'd obviously realized his daughter had mispronounced.

"Bethany," Meg clarified.

Logan nodded and it was enough to send a whiff of his ocean-air-smelling cologne to her—the scent that had announced that he'd also showered and shaved for tonight. Showered and shaved and changed into a pair of dark denim jeans and a baby-blue polo shirt that accentuated his eyes and made it difficult for Meg not to get lost in staring into them…

"So, Tia had a good time," he concluded.

"I'd say it was a successful socialization."

"Or just a good time," Logan repeated, obviously wanting to simplify it. "And proof that Tia doesn't need a resident psychologist."

Meg took what she hoped was a calming breath. "Playgroup went well," she said succinctly.

"How about for you?" he asked then. "Did you meet up with any old friends?"

"I saw a few people I knew from school," she answered without encouraging more, pretending an interest in the baseball game that was in the final inning.

Just then a man and woman Meg didn't recognize came up the bleachers to introduce themselves to Logan, telling him that they were interested in a particular chair they'd seen on his Web site.

While he talked business, Meg zoned out, taking herself to task. Logan was just being friendly, why was it that she had to make more of that than it was? And then get upset when there *wasn't* more to it?

Okay yes, she was attracted to him. But it was no different than if she'd noticed him when she was twelve and he was eighteen and had developed a crush on him—he would have been off-limits then and he was no less off-limits now.

And thank goodness she *hadn't* kissed him! That would have given her away and been much worse to try to recover from. As it was, the worst she'd done was think things she shouldn't have thought about him, and displayed what he probably interpreted as mood swings. If she got herself under control—in a way that didn't make her sound like the keynote speaker at a psychology conference—Logan would never be the wiser.

Unless he knew how close she'd come to kissing him last night. It seemed as if he might.

But she had to assume that he hadn't. She just had to or going on as his daughter's nanny might not be possible.

Logan's conversation with the couple ended at the same time the game did. As he and Meg stood she thought that one of the things she should do in the future was not accept invitations for things like tonight. Family meals were one thing, but family outings on which a nanny wasn't needed should be things she begged off of. There might not be a distinct line between the personal and the professional when it came to this job, but she thought she should start to draw at least a faint one.

Then Logan gave her the perfect opportunity for that.

"How about a walk?" he suggested. "In all the time I've been back in town I haven't had the chance to just walk around and see what's changed and what's the same."

But did she take the opportunity and begin to draw that faint line to distinguish the personal from the professional?

She told herself to.

And yet what came out of her mouth was, "Okay. It *is* a beautiful night…"

Still, she reasoned once the words were out, she needed to amend whatever impression she might have given that she was irked about something. And a walk was just a walk—she could do that without making it into something it wasn't, couldn't she?

She was just going to have to.

"I'm not the best tour guide," she warned. "I've been back to town for a few vacations over the years, but not often enough or for long enough periods of time to keep up."

"Then we'll both get to check it out," he said as they reached the bottom of the bleachers. "But before we hit Main Street, let's see if we can get into the middle school building. I left something there."

The school campus was comprised of three buildings—one for the elementary grades, one for the middle grades, and one for the high school. All grade levels shared the cafeteria, the auditorium, the administration offices, the gym, the playground and the sports field.

"You left something in the middle school? Recently or when you went to middle school?" Meg asked as they turned in that direction.

"When I went to middle school. But it might still be there."

The building's front doors were open when they reached it and they understood why after going past what appeared to be a knitting class in the first classroom. No one took any notice of them entering, so Logan led the way to the center of the building and a bay of lockers.

"These look the same," Logan observed. "And if I'm remembering right, it was locker 56—I was sure that even if I lived to be that old I wouldn't get over Libby Weaver."

Meg laughed. "Libby Weaver? The manicurist?"

"She might be the manicurist now, but in the eighth grade? She was the girl of my dreams," he said with mock rapture as he located locker number 56.

When he did, he took a leap, caught the top edge of the row of lockers that were barely two heads from the ceiling and stayed hanging there, pulling himself up high enough to look around.

"Luckily not many things change in Northbridge, and not a lot of cleaning of the locker tops happens, either," he said as he held on with one hand and used the other to reach for something. Then he dropped back to the ground.

Meg tried not to notice his dexterity or the way his biceps bulged to bear his weight…

"Got it!" he said, blowing many years of dust off of what he'd retrieved before showing her a poorly shaped six-inch wooden heart with Be Mine burned into it.

"Like the Valentine's Day candy?" Meg guessed.

"Exactly. I made it in eighth grade woodshop for Libby Weaver, and I etched my name into it—under the Be Mine." He showed her that, too. "I remembered it when I saw Libby on the street the other day. I thought if it was still here I should probably get it back. I wouldn't want somebody to find it now and sell it on eBay as my earliest work in wood—as you can see, it wasn't a good beginning."

"It is pretty bad," Meg said, unable to keep from laughing at the malformed object. "But for you there's the sentimental value."

That made him laugh, too. "Libby Weaver was my first love and she broke my heart," he pretended to be morose over the memory as they headed out of the school building. "I made this for her for Valentine's Day but just when I was going to give it to her, I turned the corner and found her kissing some other guy. I went back around to the lockers, threw it up there, and, like I said, thought that even if I lived to be the same age as my locker number—fifty-six—I'd never get over the pain of it."

"That is sad," Meg said sympathetically. "How long did it really take for you to get over it?"

"At least a week," he said as if it had been an eternity.

"And when you saw her on the street the other day? Did you have pangs?"

"I didn't even recognize her—she recognized me. And no, no pangs. She looks good, but no pangs."

It took some work for Meg not to hate the fact that he thought the manicurist looked good.

A lot of work.

And still she hated it…

They were outside again by then and Logan suggested they go to his SUV to drop off the heart before they crossed South Street to walk Main. It allowed Meg another few minutes to try to at least stop thinking about his appreciation of his old love.

But in that endeavor she recalled something else and said, "Ahh, that's right, the Weavers. I forgot about Rick Weaver…"

"Are those impure thoughts you're having?" Logan accused as they left the SUV behind and crossed South Street.

Meg merely smiled, admitting nothing.

"Rick Weaver was my age," Logan recalled. "If you didn't notice me, how come you noticed him?"

It didn't sound as if Logan liked that idea any better than she'd liked hearing that he thought Libby Weaver looked good.

Meg reminded herself to keep her perspective, not to forget that being there with Logan was nothing but a friendly walk with her boss on a Wednesday evening.

But she couldn't help the charge it sent through her to think she'd gotten to Mr. Unflappable. Even just a little.

"Rick Weaver mowed our next-door neighbor's lawn for two summers before he graduated. Every Tuesday afternoon. In nothing but cutoffs. And my bedroom window looked straight out over it…"

"Oh, that's impure all right! What kind of a reverend's granddaughter are you?"

Meg merely smiled more and opted to twist the knife. "And if you'll recall, Rick was into bodybuilding. In fact, I think he actually competes now."

"You've kept up on him?"

Meg couldn't help grinning at the increasing level of outrage that was sounding in Logan's voice. Even if he was clearly exaggerating it and likely didn't feel any genuine jealousy, she still thought she was getting to him.

"Yep, I think I'm remembering that right—Rick Weaver became a professional bodybuilder. It's something I heard a few years ago. I don't know if it's still true or not. But I'll tell you what—for those two summers, I couldn't wait for Tuesdays. There just must have been something about those Weavers…"

"Not too ready to analyze your own youthful behavior, though, are you?" he accused.

That made Meg laugh again. "A pubescent girl in a repressed household—there would have been something wrong with me if I *hadn't* noticed the half-naked older boy mowing the lawn under my bedroom window. Unfortunately, one day when I was home alone I went outside while he was trimming and tried to talk to him. Poor Rick might have had a great body but he was so dumb he couldn't even keep up with a thirteen-year-old's conversation. It ruined it for me."

Meg thought for sure that Logan would have something to say to that that would keep this back-and-forth teasing going. Instead her comment left him quiet for a moment before he said, "Yeah, I guess we can't all be super-brains and it's a good thing for Rick that he had the body to get him by."

Had what she'd said sounded so derogatory that it had been offensive? She hadn't thought so but maybe she was wrong.

"But if what I'm remembering about Rick is right, he *was* pretty successful with the bodybuilding stuff," she said to try to make amends. "That's part of what I do in my not-the-nanny job—emphasize the strengths and find adaptations for the weaknesses so they can get by."

And now she was back to the protection of her expertise...

Maybe she should just shut up.

Then Logan surprised her with a glance sideways at her and said, "What's your weakness?"

She rolled her eyes. "Main Street isn't long enough even going up one side and down the other to get through *that* list."

"Give me the top three."

"Chocolate," she said because that seemed safe. "I eat chocolate at least three times a day, every day. And if there's more stress, I eat more chocolate." At that moment she would have killed for the thickest, darkest chocolate brownie topped with chocolate ice cream, fudge sauce and chocolate sprinkles...

He smiled but now it was more indulgent and contemplative than the joking-around smiles of before. "I'm not talking about what you have a weakness *for*. I'm talking about what your weaknesses *are*. Top three."

"That's a lot to admit to," she said.

"You tell me yours and I'll tell you mine."

That seemed fair. And like something that was venturing further into the personal than she was supposed to be going with him.

But she decided that she would rather do that than have him think whatever negative things he was thinking because of her remark about Rick Weaver's lack of intelligence.

"My top three weaknesses…" she said as she considered what to tell him. "I'm not outgoing enough— that's the biggest. It's my nature to sit in the corner or the back of the room, to watch and listen. But participating or socializing? I have to force myself. And meeting new people makes me a wreck."

"Don't you have to do that all the time in your not-the-nanny job?"

"I do. But the difference is that I come in as the person people are looking to for help, the person who has the education and training and experience to make things better. It's not about me, it's about what I know and can do for them. That's kind of my version of Superman's costume—mild-mannered, retiring Clark Kent turns into someone completely different when he gets into those tights. Give me a file full of cognitive test results and assessment reports, and I'm fine. A dinner party or a first date? I'm too nervous to eat. You can bet that I will have a candy bar in my purse that will very likely get eaten on the way home—or in the ladies' room in the course of things if they're really going bad."

"So when you pull out the I'm-A-Psychologist stuff it's because you're nervous?"

She hadn't expected him to put that together. And wished he hadn't.

"That happens sometimes, yes…" she admitted with reservation and then, to keep things moving away from that, she said, "That's one. Two, I have a crazy-strong sense of smell—"

"That's a weakness?"

"It's so strong that when I was a kid I could never eat lunch at school because I couldn't stand the mixture of smells in the cafeteria. That's the kind of thing I would fix for kids I deal with now by making sure they can eat somewhere else. And certain people have a scent to me that I just can't take—"

"I hope I'm not one of them," Logan said, sounding slightly alarmed.

"You aren't," she assured. It would actually have made things much easier if he was one of the people she hated the smell of. As it was, whatever scent he gave off did just the opposite—it made him more appealing to her.

"That's two weaknesses. One more," he reminded.

"If I find a single hair in my food, that's it for me."

"I'm not sure that should count," he said.

"Believe me, if you saw the gag reflex that happens if I find a hair in my food you would count it as a weakness."

He looked skeptical but by then they'd reached the new home improvement store that had been brought into Northbridge by his recently-revealed cousins, the Graysons. Home-Max was closed but they paused in their walk to look in the windows. It was a major change that had come to the small town.

They crossed to the other side of Main Street then and Meg said, "Okay, now you. Three weaknesses."

"I'm a big macho man—macho men don't have weaknesses," Logan joked.

"So now we know that you lie—not so much a weakness as a flaw…" she goaded.

He laughed. "Okay, okay. Three weaknesses…Tia has to be the top of the list. You don't realize how vulnerable a kid makes you until you have one and start worrying about something happening to them. She's definitely my Achilles' heel."

"Okay, but that's a given and not exactly a weakness in your character or personality or psyche so the other two had better be good."

"I'm overly sensitive about the fact that I didn't go to college…."

That was surprisingly candid. "Really? You didn't go to college?"

"Not everyone does, you know."

Ooh, he *was* sensitive about it…

"I know. I guess I just assumed with all you've accomplished that you did."

"I didn't. Neither did my business partner, Chase. It didn't seem as if it would ever matter. But sometimes it does…"

Meg had the impression that it mattered a great deal to him for some reason, but he wasn't giving any clue why. And he was so obviously sensitive about it that she didn't feel free to probe. In fact, from the frown that was marring his face once again, she could see that he was regretting that he'd admitted it to her at all so she let him off the hook and went on.

"Okay, number three," she said.

"Number three…I suppose if I wouldn't let you use chocolate, I can't use bacon."

"No. But *do* you have bacon in your pocket right now in case of an emergency?"

That made him laugh again—what Meg was hoping for when she'd asked the outlandish question.

"Wouldn't your super-nose be able to smell it if I did?"

Meg laughed. "Oh, good one," she commended his comeback.

"No, I don't have bacon in my pocket. I just have a weakness for it."

"No weaknesses for—your rule. Come up with something else."

But they passed Adz restaurant and bar then—the local hangout where everyone gathered, particularly after the Bruisers' games. Logan asked if she wanted to go in for a drink.

That would have meant being with a lot of other people rather than being alone with Logan, though. And while it was what Meg knew she should have done to diffuse the sense that this had evolved into a date after all, she couldn't do it.

So she declined that offer and they went the rest of

the way down Main Street to where Logan's SUV was parked at the school.

As they headed for home, Meg returned once again to their weaknesses conversation. "Number three."

"Hmm, let's see… What if I say I have a weakness for the nanny?" That came with a sideways glance at her and a sly smile.

"Another weakness *for* and you're just saying that to slide by anyway."

"Am I?"

Oh, the wicked smile that accompanied that!

It was enough to heat Meg to the core and leave her leery of pushing this game any further.

So she sighed and, as if she still didn't buy that he had a weakness for her, conceded facetiously, "Fine. You have a weakness for me."

He smiled the smile of a mystery man and then changed the subject. "Can we talk about this next week instead?"

"Things aren't working out and you're firing me?"

"I think things are working out great—aren't they for you? Are you not happy with us?" he asked, sounding suddenly concerned.

"No, I was just joking. I'm really happy," she said in a hurry, realizing as she did that despite the fact that it had only been a short while since she'd become Tia's nanny, she *had* felt better during that time than she had in months, that she hadn't had a single bout of fretfulness or anxiety. "What did you want to talk to me about?"

"Just that I have to leave town for the next week."

That definitely didn't make her happy…

"Oh," was all she said as he pulled onto his property and drove around to the garage and her apartment.

"It won't change anything for you—Hadley will still be home when Tia gets up in the mornings and won't go to work until you come over. Dinners will be the same, and Hadley will take over with Tia after that if you want. It's just that I won't be here."

Which, for Meg, somehow put a gigantic hole in the picture. And telling herself that was silly, that he wasn't a part of her job or her reason for being there, didn't help to fill that hole.

"Where are you going?" she asked, hoping the question sounded merely conversational and friendly.

"Connecticut and New York. I have business to deal with in both places, I have to close on the sale of my house in Connecticut, and I promised to help Chase in New York with some things for his move here. I figure it'll take about a week altogether. But like I said, everything with you guys should just go on as usual except that it'll be Girls' Club. Is that okay?"

It didn't feel okay. But it had to be, didn't it?

"Sure," she said with manufactured cheeriness.

Then, since he'd turned off the engine, she got out of the SUV before he might have any inclination of how much she hated the news he'd just delivered. News that shouldn't have caused her to feel anything whatsoever.

Or if it did, the only feelings it should have caused were relief at the thought that for the next week she wouldn't need to wrestle with her attraction to him, and hope that maybe by the time he got back she would have it conquered.

But that wasn't the case…

He walked her to the stairs that led to her apartment and would probably have gone up them with her if she hadn't half-blocked them to stop it. There was no reason for it other than that if he was going away, she wanted the cut to be quick and clean, to happen now, before she felt any worse—something that seemed to be happening the more it sank in that she wasn't going to see him for a week…

"Did you say you're leaving tomorrow?" she asked, keeping her back very straight, her chin high, facing him as if she were unfazed.

"At the crack of dawn. About the time Tia usually gets up, so I figure I'll say goodbye to her and go. But Hadley is always up then, too, so she'll be here—you don't have to worry about coming over any earlier."

Meg nodded. "Well, have a good trip," she said perfunctorily.

Logan didn't say anything. And he was looking so steadfastly at her, those penetrating eyes of his studying her face.

Could he see how much this was bothering her? If he could he was probably as confused as she was about why that should be.

Because it was confusing. Days—it had only been a matter of days since they'd actually met, how could she be so rocked by the thought of him going out of town? And only for a week—it just shouldn't have been a big deal at all. It was crazy that it was.

Then, in a quiet voice, he said, "You know, I wasn't kidding earlier."

"About what?"

"About my weakness for the nanny…" His eyebrows arched in a confusion that seemed all his own. "I keep telling myself to cut it out, but so far…" He smiled an endearingly sheepish smile and shook his head. "So far I'm not doing too well at that."

You fooled me, she thought even as her spirits lifted considerably at that admission and the knowledge that she wasn't alone in whatever was happening between them.

Logan's smile tilted slightly. "I even tried to postpone this trip," he said as if he couldn't believe it himself.

"Too bad you couldn't…" Meg whispered, the most she could do in response to what he was saying, what she knew he shouldn't be saying. What she shouldn't be hearing because it only complicated things…

"Yeah, too bad I couldn't," Logan whispered back just before he kissed her.

It was a kiss that happened so fast Meg didn't see it coming. A kiss so light it was almost as if their lips didn't meet. A kiss that was over before she could enjoy it.

Not at all the kind of kiss she'd been thinking about giving him last night.

And yet there was still enough to it to send a mini-earthquake rippling through her…

Then he took a step away from her and held up both palms as if in anticipation of her taking him to task. "I know, a relaxed family atmosphere was not supposed to mean kissing cousins," he said, reiterating what she'd said that first day at her interview.

"We aren't cousins," Meg said, repeating his words

of that day because it was the only thing she could think of to let him know she wasn't going to complain.

"But I did promise no kissing."

She was on the verge of saying it was okay to kiss her when he took another step back and said, "I'll see you in a week."

Then he pivoted on his heels and she was just left watching him walk away again with that swagger that was a turn-on all by itself.

And what could she do? She couldn't shout that he was welcome to kiss her again anytime. Especially when he *shouldn't* be welcome to kiss her again anytime. Or ever…

Which was an even more depressing thought than that he would be gone for the next week.

You definitely better use this time to get some control when it comes to Logan McKendrick, she told herself firmly as she headed up the steps.

And then something else occurred to her.

Logan could be telling himself that exact same thing about her.

Oh, how she hated *that* possibility!

And the chance that he might succeed…

Chapter Six

The day after Logan left, Tia came down with a cold. Meg and Hadley both assured him over the phone that they could handle it and would keep him informed, convincing him to go on with what he needed to do on his trip.

As a result, Meg spent the week that Logan was gone juggling a maid-of-honor's duties for the week before the wedding with dealing with a sick child.

Working at a hospital, she'd had experience dealing with sick children, though, and with Hadley's help, the week still went smoothly. In fact, the Girls' Club feel of it actually helped because Tia liked cozying up on the couch with Meg and her aunt to be pampered and watch animated movies.

The week also allowed Meg to get to know Hadley better, and she came to like Logan's sister a lot. To feel as if they were becoming friends. So much so that by the third evening, after Tia was asleep for the night, Meg and Hadley began an every-night run of romance movies, snacking and girl talk.

And yet through it all, for Meg, there was still something missing without Logan there. And no amount of reasoning with herself, no amount of telling herself how insane it was to feel that way after so little time with him, made any difference. Every day seemed slightly empty because he wasn't there to say good morning when she first went to the main house. Every dinner lacked something because he wasn't there to add to the chitchat. Every bedtime and reading of *Goodnight Moon* was a little less fun because he wasn't there, too.

And every after-Tia-was-asleep time with Hadley just wasn't the same as those few after-Tia-was-asleep times with Logan had been.

So by Thursday of the following week when he was due back, Meg hardly felt as if she'd gained any more control over her attraction to the man.

Not that her determination to resist that attraction wasn't in full force, because it was. None of the reasons to resist it had gone away. But she also wasn't going to be able to meet his return with any less of a weak spot for him, either.

Which was why excitement at the prospect of his coming home woke her up long before her alarm went off on Thursday morning, and why he was on her mind almost every minute of the day.

He still wasn't home yet, though, when she left Tia with Hadley at four o'clock to go to the rehearsal and rehearsal dinner for Friday night's wedding of her sister, Kate, to Ry Grayson.

After the rehearsal itself, everyone headed to the local restaurant and pub—Adz—which had closed for the rehearsal dinner. Food, music, dancing and even a friendly pool tournament made it a big party. A party that should have kept Meg well occupied. But the fact that she could hardly sit still through what should have been a perfectly relaxed and enjoyable evening, and the fact that she kept watching the clock and wishing things would move more quickly so she could get back to the McKendricks' place, were other indications that she definitely didn't have any more power over what was going on with her when it came to Logan McKendrick just because he'd been gone for a week.

But there wasn't anything she could do about it except tell herself—again—that, weakness or no weakness, there had to be boundaries and she had to stick to them.

In fact, she swore that she *would* stick to them.

And if Logan came back with renewed convictions and self-control of his own that kept him from tempting her with even scant kisses like the one he'd given her the night before he'd left?

All the better.

At least that was what Meg told herself…

"Daddy's home!" Tia announced to Meg at eight o'clock Thursday evening when Meg returned early from the rehearsal dinner after having given up trying to enjoy herself when all she could do was think about Logan.

Logan had apparently gotten there only moments before Meg had because he, Hadley and Tia were still in the entryway with Tia in his arms and his suitcase at his feet while Hadley looked on.

Meg had seen Logan's SUV parked in front of the house when she'd pulled in. To hide her own elation at the fact that he was finally back, she'd made herself drive around to park where she usually did at the garage. But she hadn't so much as gone up to the apartment before hurrying across the yard to go into the main house from the rear.

"I see that your daddy is home," Meg answered, working to keep her voice sounding normal when what she was feeling was the same kind of excitement as Tia obviously was.

"He jus' gotted here!" Tia informed her.

Meg tried to ignore the race of her own pulse and reminded herself of the vow she'd made to take things with Logan back to day-one—she was the nanny, he was her employer, and that was all there was to it.

But reminder or no reminder, she was so happy to see him that she could barely keep from grinning ear to ear. Not even the fact that he looked like someone who had been traveling all day did anything to diminish Meg's elation as she stood somewhat behind the family tableau and watched him listen patiently to the avalanche of information Tia was giving—all of it things the little girl had told him on the multitude of phone calls they'd shared every day that he'd been gone.

And if—between *uh-huhs* to Tia—his eyes moved beyond Hadley to Meg, and Meg thought there might have been an instant sparkle to them? She'd probably just imagined that, she thought, even as he gave her a small smile that somehow said hello without any words at all and in a way that made her feel as if something might have passed solely between the two of them...

Boundaries, she reminded herself. *Stay within the boundaries.*

But it would have been so much easier if she had just managed to get even a slight hold on herself while he was gone.

"I know you were sick—you told me every time we talked on the phone, remember?" Logan was saying when Tia began to tell him about her cold as if it were a great revelation. "But now that you're almost all better, you might want to see what I brought you."

That was enough for Tia to wiggle out of his arms and demand to know what was in his suitcase.

"Let's open it upstairs, okay?" he suggested. "And then maybe—because Daddy's really tired tonight— while I shower, I can get Meg or Aunt Had to give you your bath before I read you *Goodnight Moon?*"

The last part of that was a plea to Meg and Hadley. And since Meg was wearing the dress and heels she'd worn to the rehearsal, she was certainly not the likeliest candidate to do the three-year-old's bath.

But despite that, before Hadley could say anything, Meg said, "Hadley is getting Tia's cold. Why don't we let her rest and while you show Tia what you brought her, I'll change and come back?"

Hadley put up a very minor protest that Meg waved away.

"It's no big deal. I'll be back in five minutes," she insisted, leaving again before anything could change.

And telling herself that her motive really was just to give her new friend a break.

Not because it would give her a little time with Logan…

After a mad dash to her apartment, Meg shed her dress, hose and heels in record time and put on one of her tightest pairs of jeans and a tank top that hinted at cleavage—though she was convinced that ease and speed were behind her choices, not thoughts of drawing any kind of attention to herself.

She'd left her hair loose for the rehearsal and now brushed it to freshen it while checking to make sure that the makeup she'd applied earlier didn't need to be patched, too.

The only thing she replenished was her lip gloss, and after applying it she took one final check in the mirror, realizing that her heart was still doing an excited double time beat and that her cheeks were twin spots of pink that announced just how thrilled she was that Logan was home.

So, to her reflection, she said, "Stop it! He's your boss, you're going to give his daughter a bath because that's your job, and then answer any questions he has about what went on while he was gone. But that's all you're going to do!"

And she meant it.

She would just allow herself to bask in the fact that Logan was back, she wouldn't let things go beyond that.

It would be like sitting beside a lake—she could enjoy the view and getting to be near the water, but she wouldn't dive in.

"These are my presents that my daddy brought me and this is Grilla—he falled behind the bed at Uncle Chase's lof'. We stay't there before we comed here and I din't know it and I leaved him there so tha's why we cooden' fin' him nowhere," Tia explained.

Meg had given the three-year-old her bath, helped her put on her pajamas, and was ready to turn down Tia's bed. But it was littered with the sheepishly grinning floppy gorilla Tia referred to as Grilla, a fluffy lion hand puppet, a box of snap-together building blocks, a babydoll and a framed photograph that Meg was particularly interested in.

"Is this one of your presents, too?" Meg asked of the picture that she picked up first in order to take a closer look.

"No, Daddy said the movers forgetted some boxes and Uncle Chase is gonna bring 'em wis him when he comes. But that was in one of 'em and Daddy bringed it home now."

The photo was of a woman holding a newborn. Meg had to assume it was Tia with her mother. But she wanted to know for sure, so she said, "Is this you when you were just a baby?"

Tia was more interested in putting her hand inside the puppet and making growling noises to tease Max and Harry who had just bounded into the room and jumped onto the bed, too. "Yeah, tha's me wis my mom," the little girl confirmed.

Tia's mom.

Logan's wife.

Ex-wife.

Until Hadley had mentioned Logan's ex-wife once or twice during their conversations this last week, Meg hadn't been sure exactly who Tia's mother had been in Logan's life. She'd assumed her to be an ex-wife or ex-girlfriend and not a late wife or late girlfriend, but the subject had never come up with Logan or Tia or Hadley before that. As curious as Meg was about Tia's mother, she'd forced herself not to pry for more information. But now here she was, with a picture of the woman in her hands...

Blond and strikingly pretty with a refined bone structure and Tia's same brown eyes, the woman's smile didn't look genuine and she wasn't holding Tia the way an infant was usually held. She was sitting and holding Tia stiffly with Tia's back braced against her front, hands around Tia's ribcage as if she were holding a fragile vase up for inspection.

"You were just a bitty baby," Meg said, hoping that would prompt the little girl to add something more.

It didn't.

So Meg said, "Do you remember when your mom lived with you?"

"Huh-uh."

"When do you see your mom now?" Meg asked, rationalizing that inquiring about Tia's relationship with her mother was a reasonable thing to do.

"I see her sometimes," Tia answered without stopping her play with her puppies.

"But not a lot? Is that because she lives far away?"

"She lives in a house wis lots a books. But you can't color in 'em. She ge's mad if you do…"

Mom had a temper?

"Do you ever spend the night with your mom?" Meg asked conversationally as she gathered up the remainder of the toys.

"My bed's not at her book house," Tia said as if Meg were slightly dim to need that explained to her. "She comes to our house for a little while and I has to be p'lite."

It took Meg a moment to figure out that *p'lite* was polite. Tia was warned to be polite to her own mother? That didn't sound like a close parent-child relationship. But it also didn't seem to bother the child.

"Would you like to see her more? To ever stay with her?"

"I like my dad. He knows 'bout guh'night moon and Grilla and what to do when I sneeze—say *bless you* not *use a tissue*."

Apparently a faux pas her mother had made since Tia did a stilted-sounding mimicry.

Meg took the toys to the toy box and, with another glance at the photograph, said, "Would you rather have your mom's picture on your nightstand or over on the dresser?"

Tia shrugged again. "Dresser," she said offhandedly, more involved in playing tug with Harry and the hand-puppet than in the decision.

Tia's indifference to her mother raised a lot of other

questions in Meg's mind, but just then Logan's bedroom door opened and he crossed the hall saying, "Okay, girls, it's story time!"

"I know you're tired so I'll say good-night and let you go to bed, too," Meg offered half an hour later when she and Logan left Tia's bedroom after getting the child to sleep.

Ending the evening already was a reluctant suggestion because Meg would have preferred just a few minutes more with him. But he'd already announced that he was worn out and in the interest of keeping things on the up-and-up with him, she forced herself to say what she knew she should say.

Logan didn't disagree, which made her think he might have come home with the same resolution to maintain distance between them.

He did counter her suggestion with one of his own though. "I'll drive you around back—I'm going to move my car to the garage anyway. I didn't feel like dragging my suitcase and carry-on and the rest of my stuff across the yard so I parked out front."

Meg had wondered about his parking choice when she'd seen his car there. And while she certainly didn't need a ride to the garage apartment, it did provide her with those few more minutes.

"Okay," she agreed.

Logan held the front door for her and then the passenger door of his SUV before he walked around to his side. Watching as he did, Meg took in the sight of him freshly showered and shaved, his hair dry now from the dampness it had held when he'd joined her and Tia for Tia's bedtime story.

He was wearing a pair of jeans with a ragged tear below one knee and a plain white T-shirt—obviously dressed for comfort, he still managed to be sloppy and sexy at once—and it was difficult for Meg to believe how wonderful it felt to see him.

Which she knew she should take as a warning all in itself.

"How was your trip?" she asked as he got behind the wheel, making an effort to keep things superficial.

"I did everything I needed to do, Chase and I had a couple of nights on the town, and now it's good to be home. I felt guilty about Tia being sick, and about you and Hadley having to take care of her, though. From what she says it doesn't sound as if she suffered too much—I hope it wasn't too bad for you."

"It wasn't bad at all, it got me up to date on the newest kid movies. Besides, Tia is actually a pretty good patient—she wasn't whiney or cranky, just quiet and she wanted to snuggle a lot."

"Which is probably why Hadley is getting the cold now and why you probably will, too."

"After working with kids—with an office in a hospital—and getting just about everything I came into contact with the first few years, I've built up pretty strong immunity when it comes to kid germs. I feel fine."

"Glad to hear it," he said as he pulled his car into the garage and stopped the engine.

But it had been such a short trip…

Maybe it seemed that way to Logan, too, because as

they got out of the SUV and left the garage he didn't merely say good-night and go back to the house. He walked with Meg to the apartment steps, leaned a shoulder against the garage's corner and went on as if they'd just begun a conversation at a party.

"Chase and I were talking about that, about you working at a hospital and your Ph.D. and everything. I told him what you told me—that you wanted to experience the lighter side of kids to recharge your batteries. Chase wanted to know more details and I had to admit that I didn't have any to give him."

So he and his business partner had talked about her. Meg wasn't sure if that was good or bad. She also wasn't sure she wanted to be more open with him on this subject even though he was obviously hoping she would be.

But she didn't like that note of doubt that was in his voice and wondered if his longtime friend had planted seeds of suspicion about why she was being secretive. And she supposed that he had the right to know details about someone he was entrusting his daughter to.

Plus, if she told him what he was fishing for, it would give her a little more time with him.

"It's complicated," she admitted as she weighed her decision.

"I kind of thought it was," Logan said with a smile that welcomed her confidence but didn't push for it.

It was the smile that got to her.

"I had a bad incident a few months ago," she said, sitting on the second-to-the-bottom step as she did.

Logan came to sit with her, his back to the garage wall so he was facing her. He propped one foot on the lower step and braced an arm on that raised knee, giving no indication that he was in any hurry to get home to bed.

"I see kids with a lot of different issues," Meg continued. "Physical, social, emotional, environmental—you name it, we see it all at Children's Hospital."

"Stuff that will break your heart, I'd imagine."

"Oh yeah," Meg agreed. "And stuff that's frustrating and maddening and sometimes dangerous…"

She hadn't talked too much about this. She'd told her family as little as possible so she didn't upset them. She'd told her two closest friends in Denver who had helped her when she'd come home after surgery, but again she'd downplayed the event and her own feelings and reactions. Buried it a little, she supposed. And she'd refused any kind of counseling or therapy herself because she thought she could deal with it on her own. And she thought she was. But that still didn't make it any easier to tell Logan.

"Dangerous?" he repeated to urge her to go on.

"Sure, kids can lose it and even small ones can do damage—to themselves, to anyone around them, to a whole room. I've been trained in how to restrain them—and have had to on a few occasions—but for the most part I can usually tell when a kid is about to go off and I can defuse the situation and de-escalate before it gets that far."

"Usually…"

Logan was such a good listener and attentive enough to pick up on even the smallest things.

"Usually," Meg repeated the word that had apparently given her away.

"But not always."

She shrugged. "I'm dealing with disturbed kids. Some of them *really* disturbed."

And if she was going to be completely honest with him, now was the time, she decided.

"I had a twelve-year-old boy referred by his school psychologist—the parents and the schools had tried everything and sending him to us for evaluation was the last resort. He came in sullen and annoyed with having to be there, but he wasn't raging at anything. It was obvious from the start that he was manipulative, there were some incidents of cruelty…" Confidentiality wouldn't allow her to get too far into the pathology. "Let's just say that he wasn't a kid I was comfortable turning my back on," Meg said with a humorless little laugh, trying to make it sound lighter than it was. Lighter than she felt.

"But you *were* alone with him?"

"That's part of the job. He couldn't manipulate me— and believe me, he tried—and he didn't like that."

"So he didn't like you."

Another good guess.

"I don't think this particular kid feels anything the way you and I would feel things," she said, slightly surprised by how ominous it had come out—an indication that she was still shaken.

But she didn't let Logan know that. Instead she just went on. "Anyway, I was in a session with the kid and he was doing his best to get me to think what he wanted me to think. It wasn't working, I was calling him on his lies and tall tales and basically the game he was playing that day—I was confronting him, which is a part of what I do at calculated moments…"

Meg hesitated, having the same difficulty she always

did getting this portion out. She shrugged and glanced at the porch light on the rear of the main house rather than at Logan because it somehow seemed less serious to say it that way.

"The kid picked up a pencil and stabbed me with it."

She didn't have to be looking at Logan to know the impact that had on him because it was a jolt that yanked his spine a bit straighter.

"He *stabbed* you?"

"In the side. Luckily he didn't hit any major organs but the pencil went in about three inches and broke off—"

"My God, Meg…"

"I know, he could have killed me. And to tell you the truth, he was so calm about it, so…soothed, almost, by doing it, that I was actually afraid he might go on and do more just for the fun of it. I guess I was lucky that he just laughed and walked out of my office as if he didn't have a care in the world."

"I hope that kid isn't loose on the streets—*ever.*"

"He won't be for a long time."

"What about you? What happened to you then?"

"I had to have surgery."

"And right about then you decided you needed the lighter side of kids for a change—no wonder."

"Actually, this was months ago. I was back at work in a week."

"You weren't."

"I was. But the whole thing did start me thinking. And evaluating things. And wondering if I was getting burned out—"

"Yeah, I would think that being stabbed might burn you

out just a little," Logan said, his facetious understatement making her smile and helping to ease some of the tension.

"Actually, I started to wonder if that's why I *had* been stabbed. If, over time, I'd begun to relate less to the kids, if they weren't relating to me because maybe I'd gotten too detached, too impersonal—"

"You blamed yourself?" he asked as if he couldn't believe that.

"I wouldn't call it *blame*. I just wondered if I was off my game. If maybe I wasn't building the kind of rapport I needed to with my kids and if maybe that had contributed to the situation. I also started thinking about how long it had been since I'd had contact with kids who *didn't* have problems, and how much I missed it. I thought I needed a shot of normal. I thought I needed to just get back in touch with…well, the lighter side of kids. Tia is perfect for that."

Meg glanced at Logan again then and concluded, "That's why I'm here, being a nanny instead of a psychologist."

And it actually felt better to have been honest with him. But then there was something about being with him that gave her an all-round sense of well-being, that took away the negative fallout from The Incident. It made her attraction to him that much harder to ignore.

Logan was studying her, though, and rather than letting her last words put an end to this, he proved just how carefully he'd listened to her when they'd talked other times, too. And how much of it he'd retained.

"So when you told me about what it was like growing up under your grandfather's rules," he said, "you told me that part of why you were here this summer was to make sure you don't fall into his way of doing things—the kind of structure and control you grew up with. Does that tie into this, too?"

Meg's eyebrows rose all on their own, surprised. "Wow, you remembered that. And put it together with this." But now that he had, now that she was being honest with him, she might as well let him know that he was right. "Yes, it does tie into this," she said. "Since the stabbing I've been jumpier, more fearful—"

"That seems reasonable."

"If it stays within reason. But I started to find myself needing absolute control over situations—if my play-groups got a little wild or noisy I started to get panicky. An accidentally dropped toy was sending me jumping as high as if somebody shot off a gun. I was way too stressed-out dealing with volatile parents and rather than being diplomatic I'd hear myself being more dictatorial. I was finding myself holding back when I knew I should have been doing some therapeutic provocation or confrontation…"

She hesitated but by then she thought that she'd already gone this far, she might as well go the whole way.

"I started to worry that if I didn't nip this in the bud I might turn more into my grandfather than I want to be—all uptight and rigid all the time." Not that some things didn't *need* to be controlled—like what being with Logan stirred in her.

Meg shook her head. "I haven't told anyone this last part. I'm not sure why I'm telling you—you're probably going to think I'm crazy."

"I'd think you were crazy if you *didn't* come away from being stabbed feeling on edge and needing to get back some sense of control. But it seems to me that deciding to get away for a while and regroup—which is really what this nannying thing is, isn't it—"

"It is," she agreed, grateful that he was taking that view of it, that he was understanding while not blowing it out of proportion.

"Well, it seems to me that getting away, relaxing, re-grouping before it's too late and you end up like the Reverend, is a smart thing to do. It seems *therapeutic*," he finished, making a joke by using her terminology.

It made Meg grin and marvel at how much better she felt suddenly. "So you're okay with my using your daughter as my self-prescribed therapy to loosen up?"

"Sure. I think you're more *worried* about being wound too tight than actually wound too tight. I haven't seen anything about the way you are with Tia to think that you're acting like your grandfather around her. In fact, I heard some stories about root beer floats after her bath and letting her fall asleep in front of the television while I was gone—that doesn't sound like anything the Reverend would approve of."

Meg laughed. "The Reverend definitely wouldn't have approved. But kids need a little flexibility when they're sick."

"I just hope the fact that you could *be* flexible didn't convince you that you're cured and make you want to go back to your other work."

"You want me to stay a basket case?"

"I just want you to stay."

Oh…

He was still looking at her in the dim glow of the lights that trailed up the side of the garage to the apartment door and Meg's eyes met his, basking in the warmth in them, unable not to feel as if all was right with the world again now that he was home.

Then, without any warning at all and for no reason Meg could figure out, he leaned forward, over that arm still braced on his knee, and kissed her.

It was the same way he'd kissed her on the Wednesday night before he'd left—soft, barely there. But just when Meg was afraid he was going to end it again in a hurry—like he had that other kiss—he deepened it instead.

He pressed his lips more firmly to hers and they parted in a way that prompted hers to part, too. And there was movement—a sensual, soothing, mesmerizing movement—to go with it.

The entire week he'd been gone she'd thought about that other kiss, she'd wondered what it would be like for him to kiss her again. She'd wanted him to so badly she'd even dreamed that he had. And now he was. And even if it was still a relatively tame kiss, it was so much better than that other one, so much better than she'd even imagined…

Then just when she was really getting into it, he ended it to breathe a sort of sigh, sort of chuckle, and say, "So much for promises of no kissing."

Meg knew she should probably have registered an admonishment against breaking promises. Against the kissing. But the truth was she just wished he'd break the promise again and kiss her some more.

But she couldn't say *that*. So all she said was, "I'm glad you're back."

That made him smile a crooked and pleased smile. "Me, too."

Then he swooped in for another kiss—that one exactly like the one the week before—and got to his feet.

"You have a big day tomorrow getting ready for your sister's wedding," he said. "Hadley told me she's taking over with Tia so you can do everything you need to do for it."

"I have to start helping Kate with last-minute things at seven tomorrow morning," Meg explained.

"That means we won't see you until the wedding tomorrow night?"

Since her sister Kate's groom was Ry Grayson, Logan, Hadley and Tia had been invited to the wedding of their newest family member.

"Hadley said she didn't mind," Meg said. "But if she gets up feeling too sick to do it, I can bring Tia with me." Although dealing with the energetic three-year-old in the process of wedding preparations would not be ideal.

"Don't worry about it," Logan said. "We'll manage without you and see you at the wedding. I'm looking forward to it."

He made that sound as if he were looking forward to it because of her.

But Meg tried not to take that to heart.

"Guess I'll see you tomorrow night, then?" he added.

She nodded.

He nodded back. But for a moment he just stood there, looking at her as if he hadn't yet gotten his fill.

Then he smiled a smaller smile than before and said, "Good night, moon. Good night, Meg," the way they had to say good-night to Tia every night.

Meg laughed but there was something about it that seemed private and intimate, something that made her feel as if there was some connection between them that she knew she shouldn't let herself feel.

"Good night, Logan," she whispered from where she'd remained sitting on the steps.

Then she stood, too, turning to go to her apartment.

But even when she was halfway up and glanced over her shoulder she still found him standing where he'd been before, watching her.

He waved a reflexive wave and finally set off for the house, leaving Meg only one glimpse of him before she went inside.

Thinking as she did that no amount of girl-time had been as good as even just a scant hour with him.

And that probably meant she was in a little trouble when it came to Logan McKendrick…

Chapter Seven

New charcoal-gray suit. New dove-colored silk shirt and matching tie. New cuff links. New shoes. All of it more expensive than anything Logan had ever bought for himself before.

Everything chosen with Meg Perry in the back of his mind.

As Logan tied the tie on Friday evening shortly before he, Hadley and Tia were scheduled to leave for Meg's sister's wedding, he wondered what the hell was going on with him.

Not that that was anything new these days—he'd been wondering that same thing for a while now. It had definitely been a theme during his trip, when he'd realized that he was actually *missing* the nanny he'd only spent a few days with before he'd left.

How could that even be? he asked himself as he adjusted the knot. He looked in the mirror that was over the sink in the bathroom connected to his bedroom and judged the knot too big. How could he have *missed* Meg while he was away?

He had missed Tia—of course. But the nanny?

It just didn't make sense, he thought as he untied the tie and started over again.

Chase thought he *had it bad for her.* That's what his friend had accused when Meg's name had cropped up in too many things Logan had said and—according to his partner—in a tone and with a look on his face that screamed that she wasn't *just* the nanny to him.

Logan had denied it. But Chase knew him too well. Chase hadn't believed him.

"So you have a thing for the nanny? Good for you," Chase had said.

But Logan didn't think it was good for him.

Not that Meg wasn't great—she was. Exquisite, sweet, patient, kind, funny, easy to talk to and sexy in a quiet understated way that made him itch to see what was simmering below the surface.

There really wasn't anything about her *not* to like. At least when she wasn't in psychologist-mode. And it wasn't even that he *didn't* like her when she was in psychologist-mode, it was just that those were the times that reminded him of the gap between them.

Maybe it was too bad she wasn't like that all the time—it might help if he could keep that gap between them in mind more consistently. But as it was, when she was just Everyday-Meg rather than Psychologist-Meg, he was a sucker for her.

And that was dangerous.

"She's only vacationing as the nanny," he told his reflection in the mirror as he untied his second attempt at a knot and started over a third time. "As soon as she has her sea legs back, she'll be out of here."

Which was fine. He'd meant what he'd told her when they'd first met—that he only wanted her for the summer, that after that he would probably put Tia in preschool and maybe a day or two of day care just so she could have contact with other kids. The nanny thing was temporary, while they settled in and got the business up and running again after the move.

What he hadn't expected was that wanting Meg for the summer would end up having a different meaning for him.

Because damn if he didn't *want* want her...

He'd been hoping that the week away might help. That he might be able to cool off. To get a grip. But how was that supposed to have happened when he'd thought about her the whole time? When the image of her had been right there in his head almost every minute? When closing his eyes to sleep every night had meant seeing her as vividly as if videos of her were playing on the inside of his eyelids?

Meg smiling. Meg laughing. Meg playing with Tia. Meg bending over to pick Tia up and unknowingly showing a little cleavage. Meg at the counter cutting vegetables, her butt so tight and round he had to fight to keep from reaching out and grabbing it. Meg in the back of his mind when he'd picked out these clothes and wondered if those great emerald green eyes of hers would light up when she first saw him in them...

Jeez, what was he, fourteen?

And obviously the week away *hadn't* helped. Not even the two nights he and Chase had spent in clubs buying other women drinks, when all he'd been able to do was compare each and every other woman to Meg and find them lacking.

"She's a *doctor* of psychology. Eventually you are going to bore her," he told his reflection.

But right now?

Right now the wheels were definitely beginning to turn. One look at her coming in from the back of the house last night and it was as if someone had turned on the sun just for him. It didn't matter that he'd been traveling all day. It didn't matter that he was tired and a little hungover. Nothing had mattered but that Meg was there.

One look at her and all he could think was that he had to come up with some reason to have even just a few minutes alone with her.

That's when he'd known for sure that the trip hadn't done a single thing to help cool him off. That and when just sitting with her on the steps, talking with her, had been a better time than either of those nights clubbing with Chase and the bevy of women his friend attracted.

Nothing could compete with just being with Meg, being able to look at that delicate, porcelain-perfect face and feel the warmth of her nearby, and hear the sound of her voice again.

Oh yeah, he had it bad for the nanny...

So what was he going to do about it? he asked himself as he decided the third knot in his tie could stay.

He knew what he should do—he should tell her he'd decided he didn't need a nanny after all and send her away before things went any further than they already had.

It was a solution. A firm and final solution that meant that whatever it was that kept pulling him toward her wouldn't be able to pull him toward her any more. He'd be saved from ever reaching the point where he bored her.

But there was just no way in hell he was going to do it.

"So you'll just let things happen and suffer the consequences?" he asked his reflection scornfully.

The answer was yes, that was exactly what he was going to do, the risk he was going to take. Because the only way to stop it was to send Meg away and he couldn't make himself do that.

"Then you get what you get," he told his reflection. "If you don't do what you need to do to protect yourself, you're gonna get leveled. Again."

Maybe he was as stupid as he'd been taken for in the past.

Or maybe he could just go with what Chase thought—Chase thought this was nothing but a little infatuation with the first woman who had roused anything in him since Helene. Chase thought he should simply go with the flow, knowing that in a short while Meg would move on.

He and Chase had done plenty of that in the old days when they'd traveled around the country, never staying in any one place for too long. The fact that now it would be Meg moving on instead of him didn't matter, the principle was still the same—whatever went on between them was a temporary thing, he could enjoy it while it lasted, and not make anything more of it than it was.

He hadn't agreed or disagreed with Chase when his partner had suggested it, he'd merely changed the subject. But now he thought *why not?*

Meg was an adult who also knew their time together had a limit. Even Tia knew Meg wasn't a permanent fixture. And Meg hadn't balked either time he'd kissed her. In fact, the night before he'd kissed her that first time he could have sworn *she* was going to kiss *him.*

So what was the harm in enjoying Meg's company while she was here? He hadn't met any woman whose company he'd enjoyed this way since his divorce, he hadn't really dated, he hadn't done anything but be a single dad and keep his nose to the grindstone. Hadn't he earned a little…well, whatever this was? Sitting outside on summer nights talking, kissing, maybe dancing with her at her sister's wedding tonight…

Dammit, he thought he *had* earned it. And he was going to stop making a bigger deal out of it than it was. So he liked the nanny, so what?

And hell, he might even manage *not* to bore her in the short run.

But even if he did, what was the worst that could come of it? That she'd go back to Denver and a life he had no doubt was full of other psychologists and doctors and educated people who could keep her Ph.D. muscles toned? She was going to do that anyway. If he bored her sooner rather than later and she left early, there was nothing he could do about that.

But in the meantime, he could just ride this infatuation train as far as it went. No harm, no foul…

"Daddy! Daddy! Lookit me! I look like a pitty lady!"

Logan stepped out of the bathroom. There was nothing ladylike about the way Tia bounded into his bedroom then.

"Lookit!" the three-year-old demanded when she stopped in the center of the room and twirled around.

He knew that Meg and Hadley had taken Tia shopping for the occasion but this was the first he'd seen of his daughter's new dress. It was blue taffeta with brown polka dots and a brown sash that separated the top from the full, ankle-length skirt.

"This can't be my Tia," Logan said. "This must be someone else. Some pretty, pretty lady who Aunt Had let in."

"Uh-uh, iss me!" she said with delight.

"Hold still so I can see for sure," he said to stop the twirling before she got dizzy and fell.

Tia went into an instant freeze, posing like a statue. "See? Iss me!"

"It is you! And you are the most beautiful little girl I have ever seen!"

Tia puckered up her lips as if in an exaggerated kiss to display them, too, talking that way. "And lookit—I gots on lisstick."

As far as Logan could tell, his sister must have applied some gloss. "Beautiful, just beautiful," he assured. "You even let Aunt Had put barrettes in your hair?"

"They goes wis the dress," Tia said matter-of-factly of the hair adornments that she usually wouldn't allow to contain her curls.

Then, as if reciting something she'd been coached to say, she added, "An' Had tole me to say she's waitin' downstairs."

Logan held out his hand for his daughter to take. "I guess we better get going then," he said.

But it wasn't his daughter's or his sister's urging that really caused his eagerness to leave.

Now that he'd made up his mind to roll with whatever it was that was happening with Meg, he couldn't wait to get to her....

Meg thought that her sister Kate's wedding was like Kate herself—the ceremony was elegant and serious the way Kate was on the surface, the reception was a little on the wild side like the underlying Kate.

Their stoic grandfather performed the service in the flower-bedecked living room of Theresa Grayson's house, then stood back to scowl at the picnic-fare food that was served under a tent outside while a local rock band kept things lively.

Theresa Grayson had only attended her other two grandchildren's recent weddings from behind the scenes, watching the ceremonies at a distance where she couldn't be seen herself. But the persuasive talents of Ry Grayson and the presence of Logan, Hadley and Tia convinced even the reticent Theresa to make an appearance at this one. Tia, in particular, drew out the elderly woman, but Meg thought that was understandable— who could resist Tia's delight at being there in her first party dress?

But by nine o'clock Theresa and her caregiver, Mary

Pat, had disappeared, and an overly tired Tia was turning cranky. Since the cake had been cut and served, Hadley—who was feeling progressively sicker—suggested that she take Tia home, and that Meg drive Logan back later.

Tia didn't like that idea but, while Meg looked on, Logan carried the three-year-old out to his SUV anyway, buckled her into her car seat and bid her and the moon good-night.

Which then left Logan all to Meg...

At least that was how Meg saw it.

They hadn't made any kind of formal date for the evening but from the moment the wedding ceremony ended, they'd been together as if they had. With Hadley and Tia. But now Hadley and Tia were gone...

Meg had been feasting on the sight of Logan all evening and as he watched his sister drive off with his daughter and then rejoined Meg, Meg again devoured the sight of him in a suit that fit him to a T. His strong, straight back and broad shoulders made the perfect hanger for the jacket, and the pants accentuated the length of his legs and only hinted at the massiveness of his thighs.

His hair was rakishly sexy tonight, he smelled wonderful, and Meg wished her sister had chosen a band that played soft, slow music so she could dance in those powerful arms of his.

But as it was, when he smiled and said, "How about a dance?" that meant diving into the fast dancing going on behind the house, not dancing in his arms.

Still, she would be with him, Meg reasoned. And

while she told herself that now that the need to help with Tia was gone she should mingle rather than focusing on Logan alone, that didn't make her actually do it. Instead she just said, "Sure," as they returned to the reception.

And dance they did, though only twice before the music was suspended so Kate could toss the bouquet.

After that the band started up again even louder and more stridently than before and the older guests began to leave. Meg found herself wishing she and Logan could, too.

So when—after Meg missed catching the bride's bouquet—Logan leaned close to her ear and asked if she wanted to dance again, Meg answered, "Actually, unless you want to stay, I wouldn't mind leaving…"

Logan grinned as if she'd read his mind and they began to say their goodbyes so they could make an exit.

Meg's car was parked in the Graysons' driveway and halfway there she paused. "I can't go another step in these shoes or I might die," she said, slipping off the three-inch heels that went with the drop-waist, knee-length yellow chemise that all the bridesmaids had worn.

"You're gonna drive barefoot?"

"Unless you want to."

"Not barefoot, but I'd be happy to drive," he offered.

Meg handed him the keys and they went the rest of the distance to her car.

There was something liberating about being barefoot, about having the day and the wedding behind her, and Meg ignored her safety belt and sat angled in the passenger seat with her legs tucked under her.

"Home, driver," she ordered when Logan was behind

the wheel. She knew she was going to regret it if they got to his place and the evening ended. But she was hoping that it wouldn't. That instead they might sit on the steps to her apartment the way they had other nights. And that was so much more what she wanted to do than stay in the blaring music of the reception.

But apparently Logan had other ideas because with an air of command, he answered her by saying, "I don't think so. I have the perfect solution to those sore feet of yours."

"Anything that doesn't involve listening to that band!" Meg said as if the group had been bad when they hadn't been.

Logan cast her a smile as he backed out of the driveway. "The music got to you?"

"It's just been a long day and it was sooo loud."

"It was a nice wedding, though," he said as he headed farther out South Street into the countryside.

"It was," Meg agreed. "And getting married is what Kate has always wanted. I'm happy for her."

"What about you? Isn't it something you've always wanted?"

Meg shrugged, resting her head on the headrest in order to look at his sculpted profile as if that wasn't what she was trying to do. "I've concentrated more on my education and career. But from the time Kate was a teenager, she just wanted to be married and have a family. She kept thinking she was getting there with other guys, but they were only stringing her along. I'm glad she finally found someone who wasn't."

They were well outside of Northbridge proper by

then and Meg said, "Are we going somewhere special or just driving?"

"We're going right—" he slowed the car, switched to the bright lights to find a dirt road that was so rustic it almost wasn't a road at all "—here," he finished as he turned onto it.

"Isn't this the Pritick place?" Meg asked when she had her bearings.

"Old man Pritick, yep," Logan said. "Who still lives here, according to my sources."

The old farmhouse wasn't visible from there so she took his word for it.

"If this is still Pritick's private property, though, should we be here?" Meg asked.

"Probably not," Logan admitted. "But in the summers when Chase was fed up with old man Pritick and I couldn't take any more of my stepmother, Chase would say he was spending the night at my house and I'd say I was staying at his, and we'd camp by the lake. Pritick never knew we were out here, so we'll take our chances that he won't now, either."

Logan drove right up to the lake and the small boat dock that went out into it. Then he turned off the car and the lights.

"It's a great big footbath," he told her, getting out of the car.

Meg wasn't sure about trespassing but she ignored her qualms and got out, too.

Logan took off his suit coat, tossing it over the seat back and removed his tie to get more comfortable. So Meg leaned her back to her side of the car, discreetly rolled down her pantyhose and shed them, too. By the time she turned to him again he'd unbuttoned his collar button and rolled his sleeves to the elbows.

His shoes were still on, though, when she met him at the front of the car.

"What about those?" she asked, pointing at them.

"It's not me who has sore feet," he said, leading the way out to the end of the squeaky wooden pier.

Her feet really were killing her so when they reached the end she didn't hesitate to sit and dangle them over the edge into the cool water.

"Ahhh, you don't know what you're missing," she sighed.

Logan merely smiled and sat beside her, angled slightly toward her, slightly toward the lake, one of his long legs curved against the deck, the other bent at the knee to brace his elbow.

"Is Chase Mackey related to Homer Pritick?" Meg asked then.

"The Priticks were his foster family—no relation. And no warm memories. At least not after Mrs. Pritick died."

Logan didn't offer any more information on the subject so Meg didn't explore it. Instead she said, "When will he be coming here?"

"Chase? It's looking like it might not be until autumn now. He still has some things to wrap up in New York and we're closing our Connecticut showroom to set up here—he has to oversee packing the whole place into a truck yet and then he'll drive it all cross-country."

"Why not just hire movers?"

"Paranoia, I guess. We want to make sure everything

gets here and gets here undamaged, so we thought it was better if one of us did it."

Meg nodded. "I suppose it would be a pretty big coup to take off with a truck full of Mackey and McKendrick furniture prototypes."

He didn't confirm that but Meg had logged on to their Web site out of curiosity while he was gone and knew that nothing from Mackey and McKendrick Furniture Designs was cheap. She'd also done some research and read more than merely the hometown newspaper article on Logan, Chase and their business. She'd pored over a number of reviews and other newspaper and magazine articles that touted their pieces as world-renowned functional art.

"How did you get into this business in the first place?" she asked then, one of many things she'd come away from the Internet search curious about.

"When we were kids, Chase and I wanted out of here," he said a bit wryly. "As soon as we graduated from high school we put what we could carry in a couple of duffel bags and took off—we figured we'd travel and have some adventures."

"Did you have adventures?"

"We had some good times, but adventures? Not so much," he answered with a laugh. "It was mostly hitch-hiking from one place to another, finding whatever work we could get and soaking things in until we felt like moving on."

"Soaking things in?"

"Sure, you know—beaches and mountains, big cities and backwaters that make Northbridge *look* like a big city. We got a taste of what it was like to live where it rains instead of snows, where it's sunny all the time. We tried out different foods, different—"

"Women?"

"Those, too," he admitted with another laugh. "There weren't really *adventures,* the adventure was just in being on our own, doing whatever we pleased, whenever we pleased, checking things out."

"How did that translate into furniture-making?"

"We did more jobs than you can imagine—food service, ranching, parking cars, fishing, lifeguarding, operating ski lifts in Vail—anything we could do to support ourselves. But in North Carolina we worked in some of the furniture factories and actually found our niche."

"Both of you?"

"Chase and I have always been more like brothers than friends—as alike as if we were blood—so yeah, both of us. It probably didn't hurt that we'd been nomads for about seven years by then and we were both okay with settling in a little. So that's what we did, and we learned a lot about making furniture. But factory work wasn't what either of us saw for the long haul and when we'd had our fill we went north—"

"To New York?"

"To New York. Where we *really* didn't want to do factory work. But we still had the furniture bug, we'd both been sketching some things, and New York was a good place to explore the artsy side of it, so we just thought why not give it a try—we didn't have anything to lose."

"And Mackey and McKendrick Furniture Designs was born?"

"Not overnight, but ultimately, yes."

"Then you conquered New York, moved on to Connecticut and now you're out to take over Northbridge, too?" she teased.

"I'm the only one of us who moved to Connecticut and that was personal, not business. We just opened a workshop and showroom there because I ended up being there so much while Chase stayed strictly in New York. And as for being out to *take over* Northbridge? Coming back here was just something we decided to do when we felt like we'd been away long enough. When we both realized that—good or bad—it was still home and since we needed to make some changes, we might as well make them in this direction."

It seemed obvious that he didn't want to outline why he and his partner had decided they needed to make some changes so Meg left him that morsel of privacy and said, "And Hadley came to do the upholstery portion of the furniture—from *Paris.*"

"Hadley was ready for a change, too."

Which Hadley had told Meg herself last week, confiding in her about a bad experience with a man.

But Meg wasn't sure how much Logan knew—and didn't know—about his sister's love life and she didn't want to inadvertently say anything she shouldn't. So instead she said, "I hardly remember Chase Mackey, either."

"You'll like him—everybody does," Logan assured.

"Is he married?"

Logan nudged her shoulder with his elbow. "Why? Did your sister's wedding give you ideas?"

The only ideas she had were about Logan. Not that she was going to say *that*...

"Just curious," she said with a coyness that she hadn't intended.

It made Logan grin. "No, Chase isn't married but you might have to fight Hadley for him."

Nowhere in her girl talk with Hadley had there been any indication of that.

"Why?" Meg asked, slowly moving her feet back and forth through the water.

"Hadley had a *huge* crush on Chase when we were young."

"Really? His name came up a few times while you were gone but not in any way that hinted that he was anything but your friend and business partner."

"Chase never knew it, but she was nearly obsessed with him."

"And now—"

"Yeah," Logan guessed what she was thinking, "now she'll be working with us and living *communally* with the guy she worshipped like a rock star when she was a kid."

Meg didn't think she was ever going to live down her reaction to his comment on communal living that first day.

She opted not to acknowledge it and pulled her feet out of the water. Swiveling on her hip, she curled her legs to the side so her feet could dry. And so she could look directly at Logan. "Do you think that Hadley isn't over her feelings for Chase?"

"She says she is. She says it was a teenage thing, that she got over it a long time ago and I shouldn't give it a second thought."

"But you aren't so sure."

"Their paths haven't crossed since Chase and I left Northbridge. Hadley and I kept in touch by phone and e-mail but we only saw each other three times all those years because I was traveling around and she lived in Europe. It was two funerals and our father's heart attack that got us both in the same place at the same time, and Chase didn't have any reason to be in on those."

"So you're thinking that since Hadley hasn't even set eyes on him, there hasn't ever been a test of whether or not her crush on him could be re-sparked."

Logan confirmed that with a tilt of his head. "I guess we'll see. All I know is that those things can sometimes have a will of their own…"

Was he speaking for himself or letting her know that he was aware of what he could rouse in her?

Because he *was* rousing things in her right at that moment when he raised an index finger to her face to smooth a stray wisp of her hair back and that simple, light trail left her skin atingle.

What had they been talking about?

Meg couldn't recall and she had the sense that whatever it was, Logan wasn't thinking about it anymore either. Not when he was looking deeply into her eyes, smiling a small, secret smile.

Not when he said, "Did I tell you how beautiful you look tonight?"

Meg liked hearing it even though she wasn't comfortable with compliments. She never knew what to say to them. "Kate will be happy to know she didn't choose dresses that made us look ugly."

Logan smiled again, as if he knew she was deflecting the flattery, and brought his hand up again to slip around to the back of her neck at the same moment that he leaned forward and kissed her.

There was something very different in the way he did it tonight. Right from the beginning his lips were parted, his mouth, his every action was more commanding, more bold. There was no easing into this kiss, no hesitation, no reticence. It was an all-out, no-holds-barred, he-wanted-to-kiss-her-and-he-was-kissing-her kiss that sent his tongue to make a move, too.

She didn't know what had changed. She didn't really care because she was instantly lost in that kiss, carried away by it as he sought out her tongue and played a sensuous game of cat and mouse.

The hand at her nape moved down to her back and his other arm came around her, pulling her toward him.

Her hands pressed against his chest, savoring the feel of hard muscle beneath the smoothness of his shirt as she answered that kiss with an abandon of her own that surprised her.

He laid her onto the dock then, stretching out beside her, above her enough to go on kissing her, plundering her mouth with his.

Meg's hands went around to his broad shoulders, to his head, combing her fingers into his hair, all the while meeting and matching that tongue in a kiss that was out of control. A kiss that she never knew she was capable of.

Logan's hand was riding her side, her hip. The warmth of his skin seeped through the thin chiffon of her dress and radiated from every touch, making her want more of it, more of him.

Skinny-dipping popped into Meg's mind. She'd never done it. But in this small, private lake she imagined that Logan probably had, long ago, and she suddenly couldn't get the image out of her head.

Logan naked in the water…

Her naked in the water with him…

Their mouths and tongues intimately acted out the opening scene of something that could go so much further. That could easily go to shedding clothes and getting into the drink and…

And what? a more rational portion of Meg's brain asked.

Was she really going to strip off her clothes and go skinny-dipping with this man?

There was a part of her that was slightly embarrassed just to have thought about it. And no, of course she wasn't going to do it!

Kissing him was one thing—one very big thing, especially the way they were kissing at that moment. But doing anything else? That would be insane…

As if Logan sensed the sudden rise of her inhibitions he began to draw their kiss to a close. His tongue did a final pirouette with hers and bid it adieu. After a moment, he returned for another lingering but more chaste kiss. And then he raised his head and merely peered down at her.

"I don't suppose we want old man Pritick coming out here and catching us like this," he said.

"I don't suppose we do," Meg agreed, sounding reluctantly resigned.

Logan sat up and took her with him. Then he stood and with a hold of both of her hands, he brought her to her bare feet, too.

"It was a good footbath, though," Meg said. *And an amazing kiss...*

"I'm glad," Logan answered with a lopsided smile.

Back in her car, Logan drove again, Meg slipped her shoes on, and neither of them had much to say in the aftermath of that kiss.

It wasn't until Logan had walked her to the bottom of the steps to her apartment that he said, "Hadley bought two tickets to the party for the preopening of the bridge tomorrow night."

The bridge he was referring to was what the town was named after. It was an old covered bridge that had been completely refurbished, and the area around it had been turned into a park. The grand opening picnic was scheduled for Sunday, but there was a private dinner-dance being held there Saturday night.

"Hadley told me tonight that she doesn't feel well enough to go and said maybe you and I could use the tickets," Logan added. "What do you say? Can you take another night in heels?"

Now that *would* be a date...

So don't do it, Meg told herself.

But that kiss had weakened her will and her resolves.

"I think I can stand heels again by then," she heard herself say.

His smile this time was pleased. "Great."

He kissed her once more—a simple good-night kiss with intimacy on its fringes. Then he looked into her eyes for another moment and she could tell he was tempted not to go.

But he finally sighed, whispered good-night, and left anyway.

And tonight while Meg watched him head for the main house she thought that if the crush his sister had had on his friend was anything like what she was in the grip of when it came to Logan, he might be right to wonder how things would play out when Hadley was in close proximity to his partner.

Because whatever it was that Meg was feeling in response to Logan seemed to have a will of its own. And nothing she did could even slow it down, let alone extinguish it. It was just bigger than all of her efforts.

Big enough to send her up the stairs to her apartment thinking more about what she was going to wear the next night than about the fact that she shouldn't be going at all.

Especially not after that kiss that still had her imagining plunging naked into a lake with him…

Chapter Eight

Stone piers anchored the old north bridge on either side of the river that ran below it. The lower half of the bridge's sides were solid, the upper half had cross-hatch beams. Both upper and lower had been restored to their original rustic-red color, and they were topped off by a steeply pointed black-shingled roof.

The higher plateau of the river banks had been turned into a park with a manicured lawn dotted with benches and picnic tables. Cobbled stairs allowed easy access to the banks of the river itself where walkways had been added and more benches looked out over the lazy, rambling waterway.

Altogether the old bridge was judged a successful re-furbishment and the park a welcome addition to the outskirts of Northbridge. Certainly Meg was impressed by what had previously been a run-down, dilapidated, rickety old bridge surrounded by an overgrowth of weeds. For the occasion of the prelaunch dinner-dance the entire bridge and everything around it was lit with tiny white lights. Plus, for the party, there were linen-covered, candle-lit dining tables set up from one end of what had formerly been the roadway—and was now another walkway—across the bridge to the other side. There were bistro chairs around the tables, tuxedoed waiters attending to each table, and a dance platform set up on part of the grassy knoll where a string quartet played music.

The kind of music Meg had wished for the night before—slow and lilting.

The kind of music that now had her dancing in Logan's arms after dinner.

"So you *own* a tuxedo," Meg said as they swayed under the stars along with a large portion of North-bridge's natives and newcomers.

The event was formal and luckily Meg had brought something with her that worked for that level of dress-up. In order to be prepared for anything—because she was unsure what kind of celebrations might be held for her sister's wedding—she'd bought a pair of black silk slacks and a loose-fitting sleeveless black sequined top that had a flowing cowl neckline in front and a much deeper cowl dip in back that left her bare almost to the waist. She'd also brought another pair of high heels—these not quite three inches and much more comfortable than the bridesmaid's shoes of the previous evening. Plus she'd done her hair in a loose knot that left a lot of come-hither wisps around her face to make sure she looked fancy enough for a semi-formal affair.

But she hadn't expected to find Logan in a very sophisticated and perfectly tailored tuxedo when he'd come to pick her up. A tuxedo that he'd said was his when she'd marveled at the quality and fit of what she assumed was a rental.

They'd been sidetracked then, though, and this was the first chance Meg had had to ask how it was that he possessed such a formal set of clothes.

"I mean, of course you need a few good suits for the business end of your work—I figured that's what last night's suit was," she continued. "But your own tuxedo?"

"It's my I-was-a-movie-star tux. Chase has one, too. It came with learning how to dance and our sole stint as movie stars," he said with a grin.

Since most men she knew were anti-dancing—and even the ones who weren't, weren't as good at it as Logan was—she'd wondered where he'd learned and had intended to ask that, too. So he'd merely opened a door she was about to knock on anyway. But the movie-star stuff? That had her curious.

"A tux that came with learning how to dance and a stint as a movie star—that's a story I think I need to hear."

The widening of his grin said he was happy to tell it.

"It goes without saying that one of the places Chase and I wanted to check out when we left Northbridge was L.A.—sun, sea, surf, beach bunnies…"

"Uh-huh, it does go without saying that two young guys would want to check all of that out," Meg agreed.

"Well, we lived in a cheap apartment complex where a lot of wannabe actors and actresses also shared places."

"Did you and Chase want to act?"

That made him grin again. "No, neither of us had any interest in that—"

"Your interest was just in the girls who wanted to be actresses."

He merely went on grinning to confirm that. "Anyway," he continued, "one of those actresses—who was also a dancer and singer and was hot for Chase—got a part in a movie that was hiring a huge number of extras. They needed them for background dancing—"

"You were a chorus boy?" Meg teased.

He smiled but wasn't ruffled. "They needed extras for scenes where there were couples dancing behind the actors at a party, at a country club, that kind of dancing. The money was better than we were making at the car wash where we were working at the time, so we took Chase's girlfriend up on her offer to teach us to dance. Then she put in a good word for us with casting. We got hired, and the tuxes were for the country-club scene. And since I had started seeing the wardrobe girl by the time we were finished—and since the tuxes had been altered to fit us—she let us get away with not returning them."

"So you weren't movie *stars,* you were movie *extras,*" Meg amended.

"But movie stars sounds so much cooler," he said, grinning again and obviously not taking himself too seriously.

"What was the movie?" Meg asked.

He told her. "But even we can't find ourselves in the

crowd when we watch it. If we didn't get away with the tuxes we wouldn't have anything to show for it. Except the rent that month."

"And it didn't give you the acting bug?"

He laughed. "Nope. We had fun doing the one, but the tuxes were the best part of it and that was enough for both of us."

"Well, the tux seems to have made an impression on Kate's and my former babysitter Marcy Carson," Meg said when she caught the other woman openly staring at Logan as she'd done for most of the evening.

Logan didn't take his eyes off Meg to look in the other woman's direction. "Yeah, Marcy Carson…" he said with a sigh. "I've been wondering all night if she's gonna throw a plate at me or jump my bones."

That made Meg laugh. "Really? I know she's been more interested in you than in anyone else tonight, but I just thought it was—" because he looked so amazing. She didn't want to say that, though, so she said, "The tux. Throwing a plate at you or jumping your bones— that sounds like there's more to tell on that score, too."

"Marcy is a year older than I am but we were off and on through most of high school."

"She's an old *girlfriend*…" Meg said. So that explained some of the other woman's rapt interest.

"I guess. If off and on counts as that."

"It doesn't sound as if it does for you."

He shrugged the broad shoulder she had her hand on and leaned close enough to whisper in her ear, "Marcy could use some therapy."

"Sorry, I only work with kids," Meg joked as if he'd

been trying to enlist her.

She had known Marcy Carson as her babysitter and in that role, Marcy hadn't seemed any different than any babysitter she'd had as a child. Meg hadn't kept up with her when Marcy's babysitting services had no longer been required or since leaving Northbridge.

"I don't know anything about her," she said softly, in answer to his whispering to make sure no one overheard them. Plus, after the confidence that had brought his mouth to her ear, he'd left the side of his jaw resting against the side of her head and between the effects of that and the effects of having his hand against her bare back, the soft voice was all she could muster.

"I don't know anything about her now, either," Logan admitted quietly as they swayed to the music. "But I know that when we were kids, she went back and forth between…uh, hooking up with me, and throwing eggs at my house and vandalizing my locker and slashing the tires on my car and a lot of other pretty nasty things."

"Let me see if I have this straight—the *on* part of things was the *hooking up* part—"

"Right."

"Meaning that you slept with her?"

"Meaning that things would start between us because she'd sort of pursue me—we'd be in the same group at the movies and she'd make sure she sat next to me. Or she'd arrange to be my partner on some school project. Or she'd look for an opening when a bunch of us were out at the lake or at a party or wherever to talk to me and flirt with me, and have her hands all over me, and sort of go to work on me. And before I'd know it, we'd be seeing a lot of each other," he said diplomatically, leaving Meg to her own conclusion about whether or not he'd slept with her former babysitter.

"Okay. And then I assume you would break up," she said to encourage him to go on.

"And then we'd break up because even though things would start out okay and I liked her well enough, the longer it went on, the more jealous and possessive she would get, until I'd start to feel as if she wanted us to be joined at the hip."

"Which would prompt the off part…?"

"When she'd do those other things."

"Until you went back with her?" Meg asked in disbelief.

"No, that's when I'd think she was crazy. Then she'd stop the fatal-attraction stuff after a while, I'd just see her around, we'd say hello, she'd be dating somebody else or I would be and that would be it."

"Until you hooked up with her again?"

He smiled. "Until I'd kind of forgotten the weirdness and she'd start coming around me again and—"

"Then you'd go back to her?"

"Hey, a teenage boy can forget his own name when a willing girl is…well, *willing*."

"So tonight it's hard to say if she's thinking about throwing a plate at you or jumping your bones," Meg concluded.

"Either way, though, at this point, it's getting weird to have her keep looking at us like that, don't you think?"

Meg glanced in the other woman's direction from the

corner of her eye before looking back up at Logan. "I think I can take her."

That made him laugh out loud. "As much as I'd like to see that, how about if we take a walk instead and get out of her sight for a while?"

Meg was enjoying dancing with him, being in his arms. So much that she knew she better end it. She was getting tired of being under the scrutiny of her former babysitter, too, so she agreed.

They had to pass by the buffet table as they left the dance floor and without asking if she'd like a second dessert, he snatched another one of the decadent but tiny cupcakes she'd already had and adored.

Then, with a hand at the small of her back where the fabric of her top muted his touch, he guided her away from the bridge, down the steps to the water's edge and they headed away from the party.

"How about you?" Logan said as they walked, not mentioning the cupcake. "Is there anybody here who you have a history with?"

"I'm the Reverend's granddaughter, remember? There was no dating, only hanging out in groups. The first—and only—time I was allowed on a genuine date was for the senior prom and even then it had to be with at least two other couples. And my grandfather was a chaperone at the dance. And I had the earliest curfew— with my grandfather following us home and watching from the curb as my date said good-night."

"You really were kept under lock and key, weren't you? Who did the Reverend let you go to the prom with?"

"Rob Keniwicky."

"Rob Keniwicky..." Logan said, clearly trying to recall who that was.

Meg helped him out. "He was my age so you probably weren't any more aware of him than you were of me. And Rob was anything but flashy—"

"Are we talking quiet loner or all-out nerd?"

Meg nodded in the direction they'd just come from. "Rob is the guy who thought semiformal was the brown sport coat, tweed pants and white socks."

Logan laughed again. "No? *That's* who you went to your senior prom with?"

"When your family makes sure you're untouchable all the way through school, you don't have a lot of guys beating down your door to take you to the prom at the end. My choices were Rob—who my grandfather advised after bible study to ask me—or a relative."

She could see Logan grimace as they walked through the moonlight alongside the quietly babbling brook. "Was *that* the guy who gave you your first kiss?" he asked as if that would be a shame.

"With my grandfather watching from the curb? There wasn't any kissing. Rob didn't even try. He just shook my hand and left," Meg said with a laugh.

"You graduated from high school without having been *kissed?*"

His obvious sympathy made her laugh this time. "I wasn't under lock and key every minute."

"So you'd been kissed before the prom?" he asked, sounding relieved for her.

"Twice. But the first time was stolen on a dare in the

school yard when I was thirteen and I barely knew what had hit me."

"And the second time?"

"Also nothing great—it was a game of Seven Minutes In Heaven at a slumber party where boys sneaked in—which was discovered and so that was the last time I was allowed to even go to girls-only parties."

"You might as well have grown up in a convent," he said, back to being astounded and sympathetic. "So before you graduated from *high school* the closest you got to actually being kissed was the Seven Minutes In Heaven thing—who was that with?"

"Wes Riley. Who was more shy than I was and had bad aim—he barely kissed the corner of my mouth."

"This is just sad," Logan said as they reached a bench so far from the party that they couldn't see or hear it any longer.

He motioned for her to sit. "I guess this is consolation," he added, handing her the mini cupcake as he joined her and stretched an arm along the bench back behind her.

The cupcakes were bite-size brownies filled with raspberry and topped with a swirl of white chocolate mousse. Left to her own devices, Meg could have eaten at least six. But she didn't want to be rude, so after she'd accepted it, she said, "Want half?"

"No, you can have the whole thing—I *was* kissed before my senior prom," he said.

Meg wasn't about to argue and only get half of the cupcake. She did eat it in two bites rather than one, however, so she didn't make a pig of herself.

As she savored the rich blend of flavors, Logan said,

"Did you go wild when you finally got away from here and went to college?"

Meg shook her head. "I didn't—that just wasn't me. Plus my sister Kate had caused some family drama over a boy and I didn't want to do that, too. I mainly concentrated on my studies."

"Come on," he cajoled. "You didn't do *anything?* You still didn't date?"

"Not the first two years of college. But after that I started to worry that all work and no play was making me a very dull girl, so I made some time for a social life."

"Finally!" He was fiddling with the wisps of hair at her nape and it tickled and tingled at once, sending goosebumps down her arms. But in a good way, especially since he'd somehow moved closer to her to do it.

"Was your socializing in the form of dating multiple guys or long-term relationships?" he asked then.

"Both," she said. "I dated some guys on campus until I met my roommate's brother—I was with him all through senior year, but graduation ended that. And then I was involved with someone else through all of grad school and up until about a year ago…"

"That one left a mark," Logan guessed.

Meg hadn't meant for her voice to change when she'd mentioned the only genuinely serious relationship she'd been in. But it had, and she couldn't help it. She was sure that had given her away.

"Randy was a junior high school teacher I met during a practicum at his school. We were together two years." She hesitated and then admitted, "We were engaged but it didn't work out."

"Do I need to go back and get more cupcakes to bribe you into telling me why?"

She laughed, thinking that she was still enjoying herself even though they'd ventured into a subject that was unpleasant for her.

"Would you?" she asked hopefully.

"Back in a flash."

"No, I'm kidding," she said before he got more than a few inches off the bench. But somehow her hand had gone to his knee to stop him and *that* was certainly more familiar than she should have been with him!

She snatched it back in a hurry.

But even though she was embarrassed to have done it, she wasn't sorry that when he sank onto the bench seat again he was nearer still. Near enough for that thigh she'd just reached for to press up against the length of hers.

"So why didn't you marry this Randy guy?" Logan asked then, apparently taking her grab of his leg in stride.

"He broke it off. For reasons you'll probably understand."

"I doubt that."

"You hate it when I'm too much the psychologist."

"I just don't like things overly technical or formal."

"Says the man who owns his own tuxedo," she goaded just to keep the tone light because she was having such a good time with him she didn't want to put too much of a damper on it—despite the fact that he seemed determined to hear about her failed romantic past.

"I don't think owning my own tuxedo because I made off with it during my brief foray into moviemaking qualifies me as a formal kind of guy. Don't forget, I never even went to college."

She also hadn't forgotten that it bothered him so Meg didn't dwell on what she was afraid really could ruin the evening, and instead told him what he wanted to know.

"The breakup came out of a fight over something he said was nothing—we were supposed to pick out wedding invitations and he stood me up."

"That doesn't seem like nothing."

"That's what I said," Meg appreciated that Logan was on her side. "I said we should talk about it. That it seemed like a passive-aggressive way of letting me know that maybe he wasn't ready to move forward with the wedding."

Logan smiled. "But *that* sounds more like a psychologist talking than someone who has reason to be ticked off over being stood up to pick out her wedding invitations."

Meg sighed. "Randy's point exactly. He said that was the real problem—that I never knew when to stop being a psychologist. That he felt like everything I did or said came from some kind of manual for how to have an emotionally healthy, psychologically well-balanced relationship. That even when we fought, he lost his temper and yelled and screamed, and I just analyzed everything— him included. That when I should have been furious about him not showing up to pick out the invitations, I wasn't, I was just holding a clinic on passive-aggression."

"And what did you think about that?"

"I thought we were both right."

"That he wasn't really ready to get married and

had doubts, and that maybe you *had* played it too much by-the-book?"

"Yes. Not that I did what I did on purpose, but I could see where he probably was getting more therapist than partner. Where I disconnected from my own emotions and did more analyzing than really being a full part of things—"

"Because maybe you weren't ready to marry him, either, or maybe because you knew he wasn't the right guy for you after all…"

Meg grimaced. "How come everyone but you heard this and only saw what a rotten thing it was for Randy to dump me?"

Logan merely arched a challenging eyebrow at her.

"Okay, yes," Meg conceded. "I don't think I was really head-over-heels, swept-off-my-feet *in* love with Randy and so that's why I was going more by-the-book, through-the-motions, than being as invested as I should have been, as I would have been if I *had* been head-over-heels, swept-off-my-feet *in* love with him. But you're not supposed to realize that and call me on it, you're supposed to feel bad for me and say what a jerk he was for dragging his feet and ultimately rescinding his proposal."

Logan grinned. "I can't tell you how bad I feel for you. That guy had to be a huge jerk for asking you to marry him if he wasn't ready for it and then dragging his feet after the fact," he recited mechanically.

But then he switched gears, looking at her sympathetically when he said more genuinely, "I'm sure it still hurt. You must have had deep enough feelings for him to say you'd marry him in the first place and you *were* planning your future with him. Regardless of the rest, it was an end to all of that and that's never easy."

She appreciated that he saw that side of it, too. "It did hurt," she confessed with less flippancy than before. "In a lot of ways we were really good together. He was a decent guy, we wanted the same things, we'd planned to have kids and he would have been a great dad. There wasn't anything wrong with him on the whole, it was really me who blew it. And since then I've spent a lot of time wondering what was wrong with me that I *didn't* love him more. If maybe being brought up the way I was had somehow stunted me, left me lacking or incapable. Or if maybe there was too much of my cold, remote, withholding grandfather in me—"

Meg caught herself, surprised that those words had just come out.

"I can't believe I said that," she admitted. "I haven't told that to anyone."

Logan cupped a hand around her nape and gave it a comforting squeeze. "I haven't noticed anything stunted about your growth," he joked gently.

He kissed her then, but it wasn't a consoling kiss. Even from the start it was a kiss that said something else was overtaking him, too. His lips were parted when they met hers and there was heat in the kiss from the very beginning. Heat that Meg welcomed, met and matched in the parting of her own lips, in the instant raise of her hands to his chest.

She had no idea what exactly it was that was going on when it came to Logan, she only knew that every time they were together there was some kind of irresistible draw that caused things to erupt between them. Things that she couldn't deny. And no amount of reminding herself why she *should* deny them, made her.

Instead she responded to that kiss with a fervor of her own, greeting his tongue when it made its appearance, more than ready to frolic and play and counter every twist and turn, every thrust and circle.

His free arm went around her. He pressed his hand to her bare back much as he had every time they'd danced. And maybe that was the problem, because after an evening of the feel of his palm against her skin, now that they were alone, now that he was kissing her the way she wanted him to kiss her every time she set eyes on him, having his hand on her back again only made her want more than that.

Her nipples were tight little knots of desire straining against the built-in bra of her top, screaming to know his touch, too.

She sent her hands from the outside of his tuxedo jacket to the inside as if that might give him some clue, adding the arch of her spine even as he massaged her back in a sensual way he hadn't on the dance floor.

Their mouths opened wider, their tongues grew brasher and bolder. Meg found Logan's perfect pectorals through his shirt, mimicking his massage on her back with just the cloth of his shirt as a barrier.

Oh, to be wearing only a single layer! As it was, when Logan slid his hand from her back to just the outer swell of her breast, what he encountered were folds of sequined silk over the inner shell of bra. It might as well have been chain mail for all Meg could feel.

A frustrated sigh escaped her as mouths continued their rapt quest.

But Logan was apparently not going to let simple sequins get the best of him because he found the hem of her top and slipped his hand underneath.

To her waist alone at first.

She didn't know why, after an evening of having his hand on her exposed flesh, it should seem different there, but it did. Different and exciting, intimate and forbidden, it kicked up their kiss a notch, too, becoming a frenzy. Their breaths came faster, and so did Meg's heart rate in eager anticipation as Logan's hand began to rise.

Slowly, building her craving of his touch, he left a trail of glittering sensations along the surface of her skin until he finally discovered her breast.

She didn't want to moan but a very soft one sounded at that first contact. That very first, glorious contact when his powerful hand closed around her yearning breast and let her nipple harden into a diamond against his palm.

His fingers pressed into her, kneading, caressing, molding that oh-so-pliable globe, awakening and arousing dangerously delicious things inside of her, making her increasingly aware of the scent of his cologne, of the cottony whisper of his breath against her cheek, of the hardness of his muscular torso bracing her hands.

She wanted—needed—to be closer to him. To know the length of his body running the length of hers. To bear the weight of him and explore so, so much more.

But it was a scant bit of a breeze that brushed across them then that reminded her where they were, that no matter what was coming to life in her, it couldn't be satisfied there and then. And with that came the thought that anyone else from the dinner dance could take the same walk she and Logan had taken and happen upon them.

That should have put a damper on her desires. But she wanted this to go on so badly that it still took an act of will to force herself to put an end to at least the kiss in order to say, "What if somebody comes out here?"

It was Logan's turn to groan but his was in complaint before he took a deep breath and exhaled resignedly. "Yeah, I don't suppose we should be christening the park ourselves," he conceded. "But we could take this home…"

"We could," Meg confirmed, the thought of picking this up in a more private setting titillating the needs that were still churning in her.

Logan slipped his hand from under her top, took her hand in his grip instead and they retraced their steps on the river bank walkway, bypassing the party to get them to his SUV with single-minded intent.

But somewhere along the way home reality sank in for Meg and by the time they reached the apartment door she stalled.

Rather than letting them both inside, she turned and faced Logan, peering up at that handsome face dusted in moonlight, wanting him still so much she ached, but cursing courage lost to remembering their work arrangement, and transitions and upheaval in both their lives, and that there was also Tia to consider…

"Second thoughts?" he asked as if reading her mind, disappointment in his tone.

He was standing close in front of her, holding both of her hands in his at hip-height, and it was so tempting to just give in.

But she didn't.

Instead she said, "I hate to say it—"

"But yes, you're having second thoughts," he finished for her.

He looked down into her eyes for a long moment, patiently accepting without condemning. Understanding.

Then he smiled a cocky half smile that made her want him all over again and said, "Tomorrow's another day."

Meg smiled back at him but that was her only response, not committing to anything, but not refusing anything either.

He kissed her once more—mouths wide, tongues teasing again just that quick, before he was the one to end it this time.

"Nope, you're not stunted," he joked.

Another kiss—not quite chaste but keeping his tongue to himself—and then he said good-night.

And tonight Meg went inside rather than watching him go because she knew that the sight of him leaving was too likely to spur her to beg him not to.

But even behind the closed door of her apartment, when she told herself she'd done the right thing in not taking what had happened alongside the river any further, she wasn't quite sure she believed it.

Not when she was fighting the mental image of tearing away that tux he'd had on tonight, dropping her own fancy clothes, and sharing the bed he'd made with his own two hands.

Hands that she could still feel on her back, on her breast.

Hands she just wanted to feel everywhere else, too…

Chapter Nine

Meg spent Sunday morning at the main house packing for the bridge's public grand opening picnic with Logan, Hadley and Tia.

In those situations Meg and Logan didn't behave any differently than they had at the outset of Meg becoming the nanny. But despite the fact that they'd somehow silently agreed not to give away what was going on between them when they were alone, Meg still felt a sort of electricity in the air whenever Logan was in the room. Electricity that sent an extra jolt through her each time some chore brought them near to each other.

And even though they kept things purely on the up-and-up, Meg did catch Logan stealing glimpses of her if no one else was looking—the way she did of him. Plus there were a number of exchanges of small smiles that passed only between them and again, only on the sly. There was the occasional brush of their hands or arms or shoulders that appeared accidental and yet managed to rain something bright and sparkling all through Meg every time. But she honestly didn't think that either Hadley or Tia had any suspicion that there was more going on than met the eye.

"I can't get this jar of pickles open, Logan," Hadley said after several attempts. "Will you try?"

"I can do it wis my bare hands!" Tia announced, running from the kitchen.

"She had to go somewhere to get her bare hands?" Hadley asked Meg.

Meg shrugged, having no idea what the little girl was up to.

Meg was making potato salad and as she broke the boiled potatoes into smaller sizes she watched Logan accept the jar of pickles from his sister. And as he clasped the jar and lid in big hands, his biceps flexing from beneath the short sleeves of his T-shirt as he loosened the seal without much effort, Meg devoured the sight and tried to keep those bright, sparkling feelings to a minimum.

Just as Logan got the jar open the phone rang, jolting Meg out of her reverie enough to realize that her potato salad making had stalled. She started again before anyone noticed, while Logan returned the jar to Hadley and went to the phone on the wall behind Meg, robbing her of the opportunity to go on looking at him.

Then she heard him say, "Helene…" in a more guarded tone of voice than Meg had ever heard him use.

Meg glanced up again, this time to Hadley.

Hadley had frozen in the middle of taking a gherkin out of the jar to stare openly at Logan with instant concern and caution in her expression. Then she averted her gaze to Meg and whispered, "His ex-wife."

"What do you mean you're here? In Northbridge?" Logan said, making no effort to have his conversation in private, which meant that it was impossible not to overhear what he was saying.

"So you're in South Dakota on your way here because you felt like taking a road trip?"

Meg and Hadley continued to stare at each other while listening raptly to Logan's side of the call.

"No, we won't be home today," he said. "We're leaving in a few minutes for a town picnic to open a new park and Tia is looking forward to it—"

Logan was silent for a moment after obviously having what he'd been saying cut short.

"If you've been driving cross-country for the last three days you had to have known before now that you were coming through here. You could have called and—"

Another abrupt silence.

"Why don't you get a room at the bed-and-breakfast in town for a night or two and you can see Tia—"

Silence again.

"So you don't want to actually spend any time with her, you're just doing a drive-through."

Another silence.

"No, I didn't know you were getting married. How

would I know that? The last time we saw you was on Tia's birthday four months ago and you didn't say anything then—"

Cut off again, Meg heard Logan sigh a frustrated sigh, but her view was of Hadley shaking her head and rolling her eyes.

"Yes, I know how busy you are," he said with an edge of sarcasm. "But—"

The pause this time was only for a moment before he raised his voice to apparently take his own turn at cutting off whatever was being said on the other end.

"But none of that matters. This is what you always do, Helene, and I usually accommodate it. But Tia is excited for this picnic and I'm not going to disappoint her just because it's convenient for you. You can either see her later tonight when we get home, or we can arrange something now so you can see her on your way back from meeting your fiancé's family."

That seemed reasonable—he was standing his ground for Tia's sake without being hostile or adversarial. He was offering options. And he wasn't digging in his heels merely to be contrary—Meg had the sense that he would have agreed to even the impromptu appearance of his ex-wife if there hadn't been other factors that would adversely affect Tia.

After another, longer silence he said, "No, there's no reason you can't come to the park if all you want is to make a pit stop. Just don't be surprised if Tia is more interested in—"

Another silence, another shake of Hadley's head, this one more disgusted.

"Like I said, she's excited to go today so she can play with the other kids. If she's more into that than into seeing you and meeting your boyfriend there's nothing I can do about it. If you want her undivided attention, we should do something at home at another time—it's up to you."

Some understandable annoyance was creeping into his tone, but by then Meg was surprised he wasn't losing his temper.

"I can't promise that," he said then, "but I'll tell you how to get to the park—you've been to Northbridge, you know it's easy to navigate—and we'll just have to see."

Still in a level tone of voice, he gave directions from the highway exit, through town, to the bridge site. Then, he said, "So I guess we'll see you when we see you."

Meg heard him hang up the phone and stole a glance over her shoulder. He was still standing there, his hand on the receiver, staring at it. She thought that he was taking a moment to vent the understandable anger and frustration that anyone would have had after a conversation like the one he'd just had.

Meg looked at Hadley again, the other woman shrugged as if she didn't know what to do, but neither of them said anything to Logan.

Then he let out another sigh and finally came around to where Meg could see him again.

"I don't know what goes through that woman's head—" he began.

But this time it was his daughter who didn't let him finish because just then Tia bounded back into the kitchen wearing brown furry gloves that had been the bear claw portion of a costume. "I can open the pickers wis my bear hands!" she proclaimed.

"Oh, *bear* hands, not *bare* hands," Hadley said as what the little girl meant sank in.

When it did, even Logan laughed at the three-year-old who was holding her bear-claw-encased hands in the air so that the two puppies who followed her around couldn't reach them.

"Too late, Bear Hands, the *pickers* jar is already open," Logan told his daughter, who seemed oblivious to the tension that had erupted while she'd been gone. "But you know what we forgot? The sunblock. How about if you run back upstairs and get that for us?"

"Can I puts sunblock on Max and Harry?" Tia asked.

"No, no sunblock on the puppies. Just go get it and bring it to me," Logan instructed patiently.

"Okaaay," the three-year-old conceded reluctantly, charging out of the kitchen with the dogs fast on her heels again.

Once Tia was no longer within earshot it was Hadley who ventured back to the subject of the phone call and what Logan had started to say. "Helene?"

"Apparently we're being graced with her presence this afternoon," Logan said. "She's engaged and on her way to meet her future in-laws in Seattle. She thought it would be nice to drive through Northbridge so the new man in her life can meet Tia. And could I please keep Tia from *carousing* with other children when Helene and The Future Mr. Helene make their appearance because Helene wants Tia to make a good impression on The Future Mr. Helene."

There was enough of an edge to Logan's voice to let Meg know that the phone call *had* opened a bit of a Pandora's box in him after all.

"Helene didn't want to stay over or take Tia for the night or plan a visit with her on the way back from Seattle?" Hadley asked.

"She doesn't have any of that in the schedule. They're only able to stop in Northbridge because they've made better time than they expected to—she hadn't planned to do it, that's why she didn't call before. But about half an hour is all they can spare once they get here."

"She didn't even bother to say goodbye to Tia before you guys left Connecticut, and now all she can spare is half an hour?" Hadley asked.

Logan shrugged. "That's Helene. She never fails to amaze when it comes to Tia."

"And not in a good way," Hadley agreed. All the while Meg stayed out of it, knowing it wasn't her place to make any comment.

Logan seemed to be accepting the situation whether he liked it or not, however, because he said, "It doesn't matter. We won't let this ruin our day. Helene and Mr. Helene will be in and out—if they actually show up. We'll just do what we planned to do before and after, and whatever Tia does if and when they meet us, Tia does. The one thing we aren't going to do is change anything because of this."

"That seems fair since Helene won't change anything for anyone else," Hadley muttered under her breath just before Tia hollered from the living room.

"Max gots my bear hand and he won't give it to me!"

"I'll go," Hadley offered, leaving Meg and Logan alone suddenly.

When that happened Meg felt the need to say something.

"Are you okay?" Meg asked him.

"Sure," he answered as if he genuinely was. "Helene is just Helene—believe me, I'm used to dealing with her. She took me by surprise, but it's no big deal."

"Is there a formal visitation order between the two of you?"

"I have custody of Tia, Helene has open visitation that she rarely uses. So she thinks that on those rare occasions everything should be adjusted to oblige her. Under other circumstances it wouldn't have been worth fighting. But we have plans and when that's the case, plans win out over unplanned visits, as far as I'm concerned. Even if Helene doesn't like it."

He said that matter-of-factly, without any hostility or any indication that he felt as if he'd won one over his ex—things that might have led Meg to think he still had an emotional attachment to her. As it was, she didn't think he did and when he went on it was in the same vein.

"So if she doesn't change her mind," he concluded, "she'll find us at the picnic."

Logan's tone seemed to relay the message that he didn't want to talk any more about it. And since he also changed the subject to what other things they would need for the day at the park, Meg let it drop.

But as Logan packed the picnic basket and Meg put the finishing touches on the potato salad, his ex-wife was definitely still on her mind.

There were just so many things that she was curious about—Logan's relationship with his ex-wife, what had ended their marriage, his feelings for her, his ex-wife's relationship with Tia, and, certainly not least of all, Meg was curious about his ex-wife herself.

And now she was going to meet her.

The woman Logan had been in love with once upon a time.

The woman he'd shared a bed with. Had a child with.

This should be interesting...

But while the psychologist in her might be intrigued, the woman in Meg felt a little on edge at the prospect of coming face to face with the former Mrs. Logan McKendrick...

The grand opening of the renovated bridge and its surrounding park was like most of Northbridge's events—festive, cheery and well attended.

Booths offering homemade food and goods for sale had been set up inside the bridge itself. There were events and games for children only and for the children to do with the adults. There was a magician performing on the platform that had been the dance floor the previous evening, there were pony rides, and there was a teenage boy making balloon animals and hats for anyone who wanted one.

Tia wanted both and so had a pink balloon giraffe and a matching pink balloon hat that she managed to keep on her head even as she ran to find her friends Bethany and Howie from the Town Square playday to play with.

The picnic, encountering more people from their

school days, visiting the booths, and watching Tia kept Meg, Logan and Hadley busy from the moment they got there. And yet Logan's ex-wife's impending arrival was never far from Meg's mind.

But just when she'd begun to wonder if the other woman was going to make an appearance after all, Meg spotted her.

Logan's former wife looked much the same as she had in Tia's photograph. She was tall and thin, her hair was swept into a French twist, and she was impeccably dressed in white pants and a white sweater set with a blue fleck pattern in it that made Meg and everyone else at the picnic seem dowdy in the jeans, shorts, shirts and T-shirts that predominated.

She was also very straight-backed and Meg's first thought when she saw her was that she looked austere and unapproachable. Even as she spotted Logan and approached the picnic table where Meg, Logan and Hadley were sitting.

"You made it," was Logan's greeting as the lady in white led a man dressed in slacks and a sport shirt to them. And by the looks of the man's salt-and-pepper gray hair, he was at least fifteen years older than Logan's ex-wife.

"Logan. Hadley," was the woman's response, ignoring Logan's comment. "I'd like you to meet my fiancé, Dietrich Wietzel. Dietrich, this is Logan McKendrick and his sister, Hadley."

Logan stood and shook the other man's hand and if there was any resentment, Meg didn't see it. Logan seemed merely congenial.

Then he introduced Meg, saying nothing about her

being the nanny. Which Meg appreciated—not because she was in any way embarrassed or ashamed of that position, but because she didn't feel as if she was *only* that.

Helene barely allowed her a nod, as if Meg wasn't important enough for more, and then looked back at Logan and said, "Where is Tia?"

"Pink balloon hat," Logan said with a nod of his own in the direction of where the three-year-old was digging in the sandbox of the nearby play area with her friends.

Then he called Tia to join them.

"I dow' wannoo," Tia called back, not so much as glancing up from her digging.

"Come on, you have company," Logan said.

With that, Tia raised round eyes to their general area. But it didn't seem to instantly register who her *company* was.

"Come on," Logan repeated, "your mom's here."

Meg thought he must have realized that the three-year-old—who was in a sea of strangers she wasn't paying any attention to—must not have looked closely enough to know that her mother wasn't merely another one of them.

That was apparently the case because when he said that Tia took a more concentrated look, dropped her shovel and finally came to the table. But not in any hurry and not with any kind of enthusiasm or excitement.

"Hello, Tia," Helene said when Tia joined them. There was more warmth in the woman's tone than had been in anything else she'd said, but not much. And there was no attempt to make any kind of physical contact.

"Hi," Tia answered with disinterest.

"What have I told you about things like that?" Helene tutored, kindly enough but still, Meg thought this was not the best time to reprimand the little girl.

"Say things properly—say hello," Tia's mother instructed.

"Hullo," Tia said as if she were accustomed to this sort of exchange with her mother.

"Tia, I want you to meet someone who is very important to me—this is Dietrich Wietzel. Dietrich, this is my daughter, Tia."

"Hello, Tia," the fiancé said pleasantly but in no way that would engage a three-year-old.

"Hullo," Tia repeated robotically.

"Dietrich and I are going to be married soon. He'll be your stepfather."

Tia raised an index finger to point at Logan. "Hims my fathuh."

Helene flinched at that but didn't correct Tia. Instead she said, "Dietrich will be your *step*father. That's like a second father."

Tia just stared blankly at the couple, clearly unsure how she was supposed to react to that and so reluctant to react at all.

Then, as if she knew she *should* say something, she said, "I gots Max and Harry. See 'em? They're layin' in the shade."

The puppies were napping at the base of an elm tree that also shaded their picnic table.

"I'm allergic to dogs," Helene answered.

To his credit, Dietrich made the effort Helene hadn't

and at least glanced at the puppies, even though he didn't make any move to pet them. But he did say, "They look like good dogs."

"They eats shoes and dirt."

There was a knot in Meg's stomach as she waited for Helene to once again correct Tia, willing her not to. Not to make this awful, stiff and awkward reunion any worse.

Laugh, hug her, do something—anything—nice, Meg thought as if she could telepathically force some warmth into this woman.

But it didn't work. Tia's mother continued to stand there like a statue, as if she expected Tia to take things from there.

It reminded Meg of her grandfather—the Reverend would have done the same thing, waiting for someone else to make the effort to keep conversation going, offering nothing, passing silent judgment.

But Tia was a very small child. She certainly didn't pick up on the fact that her mother wanted something more of her, and after fidgeting for a few minutes, she said, "Can I go back and play?"

Helene's sigh at that was audible. "I suppose. What do we say to someone we've just met?"

Tia looked confused.

Logan rescued her. "Say, 'I'm happy to meet you, Dietrich.'"

Tia did, reciting the words without any feeling, without any real understanding of what she was saying or why she needed to.

"Now maybe you could introduce Dietrich and me to your friends," Helene suggested.

Tia clearly didn't understand what was being asked of her and again Logan stepped in.

"Or why don't the three of you have ice cream? There's a booth over there hand-churning it and I told Tia she could have a dish."

"All right then," Helene agreed.

Neither Logan, Meg nor Hadley said anything about the situation while Helene and her fiancé were with Tia at the ice-cream stand and within little more than half an hour they returned Tia.

"I'm afraid she's dribbled on her shirt but we need to be on our way so I'll have to leave that to you," Helene announced. Then she bent over, craned her head forward to offer a cheek and said, "Give Mother a kiss and say goodbye."

That part Tia was obviously familiar with because she did as she'd been instructed, and then took off like a shot to return to the sandbox, her pink balloon hat bobbing along the way.

"She's only three," Logan reminded his ex-wife then.

"It's never too early to teach courtesy and social graces," Helene countered critically, casting a wilting look at him.

"Yeah, now that we've conquered potty training, *social graces* are next on the list."

"You might work on saying yes instead of *yeah* yourself, to begin with," Helene sniped. "You're her example, you know."

Unperturbed, Logan merely smiled a wry smile and shook his head.

Then, rather than inviting Helene and her fiancé to stay any longer, he said, "How about a soda for the road?"

"No, thank you," his former wife said very formally. "But if you come to our car, I have something for you—we just came across that bottle of wine your client gave you a few years ago. I thought you might want it but I didn't know if this venue would allow liquor."

"Okay, I'll walk over with you," Logan said as he stood.

His former wife said a clipped goodbye to Hadley and a perfunctory, "Nice to meet you," to Meg and headed for the parking area with a silent fiancé and Logan bringing up the rear.

Not until they were out of earshot did Hadley mutter after them, "Good riddance."

Meg agreed with the sentiment but she didn't say it. She just got up and went to the sandbox to be with Tia.

"I'm makin' a moun'ain," the little girl announced when Meg sat beside her.

"It's a big one, too," Meg said enthusiastically, looking for any indication that the three-year-old was upset by her mother's brief visit or departure.

None of it seemed to have had an effect—Tia was merely going about her business as if nothing at all had happened.

But the encounter had left Meg wanting to wrap her arms around the child and give her the hug her mother hadn't.

She didn't, because she didn't want to make a big deal of things that Tia was oblivious to.

But she did show Tia, Howie and Bethany how to

mold sand into shapes using cups and bowls, which delighted them all.

And while to Meg it didn't make up for the poor parenting she'd just witnessed, it helped her to see that Tia was still enjoying herself.

In spite of her mother.

Chapter Ten

After Logan's ex-wife and her fiancé left the picnic, the remainder of the day and early evening went on as planned. Neither Meg, Hadley or Logan made mention of the woman or her brief, unpleasant visit, and certainly Tia didn't.

By eight o'clock all the entertainments for the kids had ended. The Battle Of The Bands competition that started then was of no interest to Tia. Plus she'd missed her nap and was getting cranky. Since everyone else was worn out, too, they put the bridge's grand opening behind them and went home.

Once they were there Tia demanded a glass of milk before her bath and promptly spilled it with a great splash all over Meg. Since the stuff was even dripping from the tip of her nose, Logan suggested that they forego doing Tia's bath and bedtime together—the way they usually did—so Meg could go to her place and shower.

She'd finished that, put on a loose-fitting pair of navy blue pajama pants with a tight white tank top, and dried and brushed her just-washed hair when there was a knock on the apartment door.

Meg had been telling herself that, after what had almost happened on the riverside bench last night, it was probably better if she and Logan didn't end today alone. And yet the thought that it could be Logan outside on the landing, that the day and evening that had been spent with so many other people might still be able to end with some alone time with him, made her rush to the door.

And sure enough, when she opened it, there he was, standing in front of a backdrop of thunder and lightning from a threatening storm, holding up a bottle of wine.

"I think I owe you an apology," he said without saying hello. "How about I say it with this?"

"I don't know what you owe me an apology for but a glass of wine sounds great," she said because it was true. Not as true as the fact that being with him—with or without wine—was really what appealed to her, but she thought she'd keep that to herself.

She stepped out of the doorway to let him in, closing the door behind him just as the first few drops of rain fell.

"Looks like the Battle Of The Bands is going to get rained on," she observed, turning to find that Logan had gone to the kitchen to open the wine with the corkscrew he'd also brought with him.

"They'll probably move it inside the bridge,"

Logan said as she joined him. "Were you considering going back?"

"No, I'm happy to be in for the night." Especially now that he was there.

Logan had showered, too. And shaved. She could tell because his hair was still the slightest bit damp, his face had lost the shadow of beard he'd come home with, and he smelled of that ocean-air cologne he used. He'd also changed into a pair of jeans that were more faded than what he'd had on earlier and a plain white crewneck T-shirt instead of the polo shirt he'd worn to the picnic. A T-shirt that fitted him every bit as tightly as the one she had on, showing off such impressive pectorals, abs and biceps that it almost made Meg's mouth water.

"What do you owe me an apology for?" she asked as she got two wineglasses from the cupboard, trying to contain the urge to run her hands over his torso, across his shoulders and down those muscular upper arms.

Clearly unaware of her wandering thoughts, Logan said, "I don't think today's divorce drama and having milk dumped all over you were in the job description."

"Actually, three-year-olds and spilt milk go hand in hand," she said.

"Still not pleasant, though. And the divorce drama definitely isn't part of the nanny's role," Logan persisted while he unsealed the wine bottle and positioned the corkscrew.

"It wasn't exactly drama—"

"It wasn't exactly fun. But it did get us this very special bottle of wine."

Was he changing the subject so he didn't have to talk

about his ex-wife and what had gone on this afternoon? Meg wasn't sure. But she didn't want to ruin this time they finally had together, so she went with the safer subject.

"What makes it a very special bottle of wine?" she asked when she'd set the glasses on the counter near him.

"A client who owns a winery in Napa Valley gave it to me," Logan explained. "She bought a lot of furniture from us and gave Chase and me both bottles of a private reserve. We drank Chase's bottle, but I'd forgotten about this one."

"Are you sure you don't want to wait for your partner to share this one, too?"

"Chase won't care," Logan said as he popped the cork. "But I'm not a connoisseur—when we drank wine with the client she talked about letting the wine breathe, and there was all that stuff about swirling it and smelling it and rolling it around in your mouth—things I'm completely ignorant of. What about you? Do you have wine-drinking specifications?"

"Just that it goes in a glass," she joked. "Other than that, I don't know anything about all those other things, either."

"Then I guess we just get to drink it," Logan said, pouring the wine.

He handed one of the glasses to Meg and she led the way to the sofa. She sat in the center while he set the bottle on the coffee table and did the same thing so that they were both at an angle to face each other.

"Ooh, I don't know anything about wine, but that's good," Meg judged once they'd each sipped it.

"I know that price was no object for Carol when it came to buying furniture, so she must have known her business. And we definitely liked the other bottle, too."

"So if you shared wine with your client—a woman—does that mean it wasn't only business between you?" Meg asked, hoping it sounded innocent enough when in truth she was fishing. Encountering his ex-wife today had brought all of her curiosity about his past relationships to the forefront. Particularly since his former spouse had been so different than anyone she'd imagined him with.

"Yes, I drank with Carol and no it wasn't *only* business," Logan admitted with a small smile. "At least it wasn't for Chase. *I* was married at the time."

Of course—why else would the wine have been something his ex-wife had ended up with until today? Meg felt a little silly for trying to use that as the opening to get him to satisfy her curiosity.

But then he spared her another attempt by saying, "I'd think you'd be wondering more about Helene than about a client who gave me a bottle of wine."

So he knew she was curious.

"Your ex-wife did remind me of my grandfather…."

Logan laughed. "That's true. I hadn't put that together until just now, but yeah, she's about as much of a barrel of laughs as he is. Now ask me the question you're dying to ask?"

She had so many. "Which one is that?"

"What did I ever see in her."

Meg laughed this time. "I won't deny wondering about *that!*"

Logan smiled. "She was different when I met her—"

"When was that?"

"Eight years ago. Chase and I had just gotten started

in New York. A big-name interior decorator was using one of our pieces in a designer showcase. We went, Helene happened to be looking at that particular display when we got there. She was telling her friend how much she liked our chair, Chase and I started talking to her and her friend, and one thing led to another."

"And how was she different then?" Meg asked.

"She was a lot nicer for one. And not her mother. But now—" he shook his head. "Actually a few years after we met I figured out that that whole persona at the beginning was really a rebellion against her parents and the way she'd been raised. But it was a temporary thing and eventually her true nature just had to come out— that was what you saw today, the cookie-cutter image of Helene's mother, Beatrice."

"Helene was rebelling against her parents just eight years ago? That's more a teenage stage."

"Yeah, but before that she didn't have much of a chance to be a kid. She's from *old money*—big money. She went to boarding schools mainly in Europe, and a small, private college in Switzerland where there were very strict rules and she followed them to the letter for her parents' approval—she said that herself. She said she was afraid that if she displeased them at all she wouldn't have been allowed even holidays at home."

"That's awful."

"My in-laws were not my favorite people," Logan said by way of agreeing. "But when I met Helene she'd just finished her doctoral dissertation, she'd been granted her Ph.D. in philosophy and she was on her own for the first time, living in New York before she began teaching at Yale in the fall. She was ready to celebrate her freedom, to reward herself—that's what she said when I met her."

"But you believed that was the real Helene," Meg supplied.

"Exactly. Plus she saw me as an *artist*—"

Meg could tell that he didn't see himself that way. "You don't think you're an artist?"

"A craftsman, maybe," he allowed, "but I'm not a beret-wearing, putting-on-airs artiste, no. Or a Bohemian. But to Helene I think that's what I seemed like—especially compared to the cultured snobs she was used to. And by being with me, she thought that's what she was being, too."

"Bohemian?"

"And that's what her parents frowned on—although I don't think they saw me as any kind of artist, they just saw me as the hick from the sticks who wasn't good enough for their daughter."

Meg arched her eyebrows as he continued. "I was starting to have some success that seemed like it would make up for not having a college degree, she was proud of her accomplishments but she wasn't full of herself—it *seemed* like an okay mix at first. And it was easy to be attracted to Helene. In fact, Chase and I were both interested in her that day at the showcase, but she chose me."

He paused, frowned, drank his wine, stretched an arm along the back of the sofa. Then, as if he was reluctant to admit it, he said, "And maybe I liked feeling that I could hold my own with a brainiac."

"But things changed?" Meg said, interpreting his ominous tone and the vertical lines between his eyebrows.

"We dated for a full year—even after she went to Connecticut to work, we still spent weekends together and any other time I could get there or she could get to me. By the end of that year we decided to get married. Her parents were on their yacht in Monte Carlo and not due back for three months, but she said she didn't want to wait, that she didn't need their permission, so we eloped—"

"And you relocated to Connecticut."

"Not instantly, but yeah, eventually I was spending more and more time there than in New York to be with her. And at first things were good. Helene said it was nice to come home to someone who didn't have his head in the academic clouds the way everyone else she hung around with did. She said it was a relief that when she was with me she didn't have to be on her toes, proving how smart she was, that I re-energized her so she could plunge back into the never-ending competition for tenure, always vying to be the smartest person in the room."

Meg made a face. "I hate those situations."

"So did Helene until her second year—when I guess she'd started to have some times when *she* was the smartest person in the room. And liked it. Anyway, early on she preferred keeping work and our relationship separate because she said I was her escape, so I didn't have to have much to do with the other professors. But then somewhere along the way—"

"That stopped being the case."

"She wanted to move up the academic ladder so she was on all kinds of committees, getting involved, and the more time she spent in that whole world of academics, the more she liked it. Then there were the outside-of-work get-togethers and staff parties and dinners that she didn't want to miss—things she wanted me to go to, too."

He finished his wine and set his glass on the coffee table. When he sat back again he said, "That wasn't a crowd for me. Forget talking movies or weather or sports—it was all Nietzsche and Kierkegaard all the time. And Helene was right in there with the best of them, getting snootier and snootier by the day, it seemed."

"And turning into her parents after all?"

"Yep," he confirmed fatalistically. "By about three years into the marriage Helene was basking in that environment and being embarrassed by what a fish out of water I was with her friends and associates. One particular night she got steaming mad at me for slipping out of an after-dinner discussion to find a television so I could get the score on a football game. I said I'd had it with seeing so much of her friends. She said maybe she liked being with them because they didn't bore her the way I did—"

"Ouch!" Meg said in response to the harshness of those angry words, understanding more of why he was so sensitive about his lack of higher education.

"Yeah, that was about where we started entertaining the idea of splitting up. But then Helene found out she was pregnant—birth control malfunction."

"That couldn't have made things easier."

Logan shook his head again. "Nope. Helene didn't want to have the baby. She'd never liked kids and she wanted to focus on her career. But I talked her into going through with the pregnancy, into trying to make things work *because* of it—dumb idea."

"But since the baby was already on the way…"

"Right. And I know I thought that a baby might help, that some kind of maternal instincts might kick in and bring out the best in Helene. As you could see today, I was dead wrong."

"So she gave up you *and* Tia." It wasn't something Meg could fathom and that was reflected in her voice.

"Basically. There certainly wasn't any kind of custody battle. Helene fought for other things, but when it came to Tia, she didn't even make a show of wanting her. Work and the life Helene had built within the Yale community were more important to her and she didn't want the distraction of a child."

"And you *did* want Tia—"

"I did," he admitted unashamedly. "I do. I also didn't want her in the kind of situation I was in as a kid—inflicted with a bad stepparent. The only way I could make sure that didn't happen was if she was with me."

He said that with conviction, and his protectiveness, dedication and devotion to his child just made Meg like him all the more. "How old was Tia when her mother left?" she asked.

"Two months. And yeah, it was rough for a while. Chase came to Connecticut to help through the worst of it but we were two guys dealing with an infant—poor Tia spent a couple of weeks in diapers that were too small for her before it occurred to either one of us that she'd outgrown them and needed a bigger size—"

"Plus it wasn't only about Tia—your *marriage* had

ended," Meg prompted, wondering about him. And any residual emotions he might have when it came to his ex.

"Sure, there was fallout from that, too. I had my bleak days. And nights. Divorce is tough." He grinned a half grin. "And you're thinking you have to make me feel better about it all. But it's okay, you don't. The whole thing was over three years ago—I weathered it and made it out the other end just fine."

Something about the way he said that made her believe that he *had* weathered it, that it was over for him. Which she was inordinately glad to know.

"And since then?" Meg asked, not all of her curiosity appeased. "Have you dated or been involved with anyone else? Or have you been too swamped with being a single dad?"

The half grin reappeared, complete with the devilishness again. "My best friend and partner is one of the biggest players you'll ever meet. He's made it his goal to hook me up every chance he gets. But there hasn't been anything serious—my first priority is Tia."

A gust of wind and rain hit the side of the apartment hard enough to rattle the windows just then.

"Geez, what's going on out there?" Logan said, getting up from the sofa and going to the door to open it and look out.

Meg followed behind, standing beside him at the threshold to watch the show of thunder and lightning through the sheet of rain that was pouring down.

But looking in the direction of the lightning show brought Logan into Meg's peripheral vision and that was all it took for her gaze to be drawn to him instead.

He wasn't aware that she was studying him rather than the storm and so Meg gave herself a moment to enjoy that view of his perfect profile.

She didn't know how it was possible to go so quickly from talking about such a solemn subject to being turned on by the simple sight of him, but that's what happened.

"I should probably make a run for it," Logan said.

That idea set off a sort of panic in Meg. It had been a long, stressful day. The evening had brought a tense conversation. And now it was as if the rain was washing all of that away, and she just wanted to curl up in his arms...

"Don't do that," she heard herself say in answer to his suggestion that he make a run for it. Then, to conceal what was really on her mind, she added, "You'll get soaked."

"I'm not a sugar cube—I won't melt," he said.

But he didn't move to go. He turned his back to the door frame and looked at her as if he knew she had other motives. "Unless you just don't want me to go..."

She just didn't want him to go—that *was* the bottom line. But what if he did stay?

Things between them last night had been headed for lovemaking when she'd had second thoughts that had stopped it. But if he stayed now, she knew she was putting them back on that road and she'd better be sure about what she was doing.

As she looked up into Logan's piercing blue eyes she reminded herself of the reasons why she hadn't thought this would be smart last night.

No, tonight they weren't out in an open, public place the way they had been at the river's edge. But there was still their work arrangement. There was still the upheaval of his ended marriage and move cross-country. There was still her own influx situation. There was still Tia and the inadvisability of Tia's dad and her nanny being anything more than employer and employee.

There was no denying it—each and every one of those things still existed and was still a reason not to take this to the bedroom.

And yet...

They were doing so well keeping what was between them private and separate from the working portion of their relationship that Meg didn't think even Hadley had any suspicions. Certainly it wasn't affecting Tia and whatever happened now didn't need to affect Tia either, did it?

And as for the rest? Transition and upheaval and flux might all be precarious times to make major decisions, but a simple night of giving in to something that had been simmering between them right from the start? That wasn't a life-altering major decision, that was an indulgence.

Of course Meg had been raised to limit and moderate her indulgences.

But this once?

It didn't seem wrong. In fact, it almost seemed like what she *should* do. What could be more of an aid to relaxing than making love...

She couldn't help smiling at her own rationalizations and the reach they were taking.

"What are you grinning at?" Logan asked.

Meg shook her head, refusing to tell him, but instead confessing, "I don't want you to go."

He crossed his arms over his chest, peered down at

her and smiled the most wonderfully wicked smile she'd ever seen. "No?" he challenged. "I thought this was where we were going to end up last night and then you got cold feet."

She was barefoot and she glanced down at them. "Not so cold tonight," she answered quietly.

He stood there watching her intently for a long moment before he reached an arm across the distance that separated them and clasped one hand around the back of her neck. "That isn't why I came here tonight, you know," he said then, his voice lower, more gravely. "I only came because I wanted to be with you."

"So...another glass of wine and more talking is all you're up for?" Meg goaded audaciously in return.

He laughed. "It's good wine but..." He pulled her toward him. "It seems like you might have something better in mind."

"I might," she answered, surprised by her own boldness and the inclination to step outside the box a little when he was standing there in front of her, so masculine, so handsome, so imposing, so sexy in that white T-shirt that left just enough to the imagination.

"Did you have this in mind?" he asked as he leaned forward to kiss her. It was the briefest meeting of parted lips, mingled breath, and not much more.

"I might have had that in mind," she conceded when he ended it.

"Did you have this in mind?" he asked as he nibbled her earlobe, the sharp edge of her jawline and then the side of her neck.

"Hmm, possibly..."

"And this?" A string of kisses linked together along her collarbone and down her arm.

"I don't know," she said with a sigh, "that all seems a little tame…"

Logan laughed. "Maybe you were thinking something more along the lines of this…" he suggested, kissing the upper arch of her breast where it swelled slightly above her tank top.

That surprised her and sent a giddy ripple along the surface of her skin.

"Yep, that's exactly what I was thinking," she lied, concealing her reaction to the fact that he'd gone further than she'd expected him to so quickly.

Not that she was having any more second thoughts because she wasn't.

His mouth met hers again, this time in a kiss that was much sexier than anything that had preceded it. He ended that kiss, too, and said, "Is that *all* you were thinking?"

"No," Meg said frankly, taking hold of his T-shirt to pull it up and—with Logan's cooperation—over his head.

She could tell that *that* had surprised him because when his handsome face was free of the shirt one eyebrow was arched at her and he was smiling again.

"Well now…" he said as if the game was on.

But that just made Meg laugh as she tossed his T-shirt onto the couch.

The game was definitely on, though, because Logan pulled her up against him and kissed her with a new vigor, maneuvering her out of the doorway in the process and pushing the door closed with a resounding slam.

His arms were around her, holding her close so she

could feel his bare flesh against the little bit of hers that rose above the U of the tank top as his mouth opened wider and his tongue instigated a sexy tango with hers.

Meg had thought his back, shoulders and chest were impressive in the T-shirts he wore, but regardless of how good he'd looked in any of the body-hugging knits, the real splendor of it all had been muted. But now it was there for her to investigate and revel in.

His shoulders seemed even more expansive outside the confines of clothing, broad and strong and rippled with muscles encased in sleek skin. His biceps were no less massive or powerful, and the wall of chest and honed abs she was up against were like steel.

Nearly tearing off his shirt had set a tone that didn't call for inhibitions and Logan was clearly not observing any as one hand snaked under her tank top and went from her back to her side and then forward to cup her breast.

Eager and intent, his grasp was masterful as he kneaded that soft sphere, molding it to fit his hand, her nipple turning into a tight pebble of pleasure as Meg fought not to writhe.

She was not alone in her arousal. Logan's mouth was wide open over hers by then, his tongue was insistent and forceful, and she could feel him rising where his hips met hers.

The man really did have a magic touch, and every clasp and release of her breast, every caress, every gentle roll of her nipple between his fingers only increased the demands her body was making for more.

His other hand dropped to the small of her back and then to her rear end, pressing her against him. A full, hard ridge behind his jeans continued to let her know it wasn't only her body making demands.

Meg trailed her hands down the V of his back to the waistband of his jeans, following it around front to unfasten the button, to slide the zipper down.

A low moan rumbled from him then, even though she'd yet to reach for him, and that ended his ravaging of her mouth. For a split-second he broke off all contact to reach for her hand and lead her across the room to climb the two steps to the bedroom platform and the bed.

Off came his shoes and socks in a hurry then, but just when Meg was sure he was going to tackle her onto the bed, he instead kissed her very sweetly and said, "Surgery just a few months ago—I'm thinking some caution is in order and I better know your weak spot so I don't hurt you."

He was her weak spot. She'd completely forgotten about the other.

"It's my left side but you don't have to worry—it's healed."

Whether or not he believed her, things still changed from there as Logan kissed her again—a slow, sexy kiss that hinted of things to come as he found her pajamas' drawstring at her navel and pulled it free.

The pants fluttered to the floor and she was left in nothing but bikini panties and the tank top. Logan lifted her to sit on the bed.

But she *was* sitting—not lying—on it so Meg was able to reach for the open ends of his jeans and divest him of those and the boxers beneath them, leaving him gloriously, grandly, naked.

He didn't seem to mind that she looked. At every amazing inch of his naked body and the long, hard shaft that proved he wanted her.

Then he pulled off her tank top, recaptured her mouth with his, and still managed to rid her of those pesky panties before he eased her to lie back while he stretched out alongside her.

That was when the warm, wet wonders of his mouth went to her breast. And while tongue and teeth and lips delighted first one and then the other, his hand went traveling.

He seemed to want to know the tone and texture of every inch of her and along the way he managed to locate her most sensitive spots. Spots she hadn't even known were as sensitive as they were until he touched them, coaxing the best from her.

Then his hand ran from her knee, up her thigh, to the secrets between her legs... He explored that portion of her while his mouth worked more wonders at her breasts.

It was Meg's turn to moan.

She reached for that part of him that elicited the same response, curving her hand around him and doing what she could to inspire a little frenzy in him. A frenzy that grew in her, too, at the feel of that iron shaft in her grip, at the ever-increasing need he was causing in her.

Just when she wasn't sure she could contain herself a moment more, his hand deserted her, his mouth abandoned her breasts, and he reached to the floor, returning with protection that he'd taken from his pants pocket.

It crossed Meg's mind to tease him about coming

prepared, but she wanted him so badly by then that all she did was will him to hurry.

Which he did, rolling back to her to kiss her once again as he brought his big body over hers.

Meg's legs opened to him and he had no problem finding his home, sliding into her in one smooth motion as if he were made specially for her, kissing her still as he pressed into her and then pulled partially out again.

For a while his tongue kept the same rhythm until passion and desire gained too much ground for anything but bodies to meet and part and meet again.

With her hands clutching his massive shoulders, Meg matched his tempo, rising and falling with him, racing with him until she couldn't any more, until what he was building within her was too great, too overwhelming, and all she could do was hold herself tight around him and let him bring her to that pinnacle. That pinnacle that exploded with more force, more light, more thunder than anything in the storm outside, elevating her to a mindless ecstasy that stole her breath and held her poised in the most incredible bliss...

And just as she reached it, so did Logan, plunging even more deeply into her, freezing there, his entire body turning to stone as that same pleasure seemed to take him out of himself, too.

Then, little by little, they both began to breathe again. Tensed bodies eased, and Logan rested his weight on Meg.

"So much for caution," he said after a moment, his voice gravelly. "Are you okay?"

"Everything is good."

Much, much better than good...

Logan slipped from her then and rolled to his back, bringing her to lie at his side this time, wrapping her in both of his arms and holding her nearly melded against him, her head cradled in his shoulder.

Neither of them said anything for a while, basking in a sublime afterglow until the sound of the storm penetrated, and then Logan said, "I'm thinking I might have to wait out this weather all night…"

"You made the bed, I guess it's okay if you lie in it," Meg joked.

Logan laughed. "What if I hadn't made it? Could I still lie in it the rest of tonight?"

"I think that might be a really fine idea," she said on a replete sigh.

He turned just slightly to his side to almost face her and pulled her even more closely to him so he could rest his chin on the top of her head and drape a heavy thigh over her hip.

Meg knew that he was falling asleep, but that seemed like the best idea for her, too, and she closed her own eyes.

Once she did, she was lost in the warmth of Logan's body all around her, in the sound of his steady heartbeat beneath her ear while the storm raged in the distance.

She couldn't recall ever feeling the way she did at that moment. Ever feeling as safe, as secure, as happy.

Ever feeling the kind of peace and tranquility that was filling her. A peace and tranquility that was so much better than she'd thought it was possible for her to achieve, even back home.

And despite the fact that she knew it was only

whimsy, as she drifted off to sleep, she had the thought that she could easily spend the rest of her life right where she was…

Chapter Eleven

When it came to furniture-making, one of Logan's favorite tasks was the sanding of the wood pieces. He and Chase both did it the old-fashioned way—by hand—and there was something about the process that was calming, that opened up his mind to do what he considered his best thinking.

And as he worked on a tabletop for a formal dining table Monday morning, his best thinking was about Meg. And the night together that had left him feeling lazy today.

Last night had been different for him.

And not because sleep had only come in naps between the three times they'd made love before he'd left at dawn in order to be home when Tia woke this morning.

He'd had more than his fair share of nights like that

to compare last night to—he and Chase had never been angels and that was particularly true of their traveling days. But not once—not even with Helene—had there been a night *exactly* like last night.

And that was because last night had been with Meg.

The table he was working on was made of oak. The top was composed of two wide planks that, while their grains were unique, blended to form a pattern of lines that were interesting and beautiful together from each and every angle.

The wood had come from separate shipments, from separate mills, from separate trees, and yet the moment Logan had laid eyes on them he'd known that they were the absolute perfect match.

That was how he'd felt last night with Meg.

He couldn't explain it. He'd never experienced it with any woman. But lying in bed with Meg after they'd made love for the first time, he'd felt as if he'd met *his* match. And that feeling had been with him ever since.

But this good feeling warred a little with his thoughts now, in the light of day.

Thoughts about the fact that being a nanny was not Meg's life's work. That she was every bit as well educated as Helene. That she obviously had to have been career-driven to achieve what she'd achieved. Thoughts about the fact that her time here was a break from her work, the way being with him had been a break from the norm for Helene when they'd first met.

Back and forth, back and forth—he went on sanding. Sanding and thinking…

In some ways comparing Meg and Helene seemed

like a joke. Yeah, Meg had started out a little like Helene was now—stiff, somewhat formal. But once Meg had gotten comfortable, she'd proven to be warm and kind and loving. And while it might be her nature to be slightly on the shy, reserved side, they'd gotten past that, too. *Well* past that last night...

So he didn't think Meg's basic nature was anything like Helene's, and that was a good thing. But the other things—the education and career focus—those had ultimately been his downfall with Helene and he could see where they could be his downfall with Meg eventually, too. He'd bored one big-brain, there was no reason to think he wouldn't bore another one.

Or was there? he asked himself when he realized he couldn't imagine Meg giving him the kind of you-are-so-dim looks that Helene had tossed at him frequently at the end of their marriage.

On the surface it had seemed like Helene's advanced education and her life in academia were what had done them in. But behind that there was also the fact that he had never been the person Helene had confided in or aired her problems or concerns or dilemmas to.

Early on she'd said she didn't want to bother him, that he was busy getting his business going and she didn't want to interfere with that.

But later, when Mackey and McKendrick Designs was out of the red and sailing along pretty smoothly, Helene still hadn't been interested in his opinions, his help, even in venting to him. By the time all the facade was down, she'd outright said that she didn't want to waste her time talking through things with someone who wouldn't understand and couldn't offer her any-thing of value as a solution.

Which meant that the truth was that from day one she'd written him off as someone who was incapable of operating on an intellectual playing field that was worthy of her, and while she might have pretended something different early on, that had still been the case even then.

But he hadn't run into that with Meg. She'd confided in him about the stabbing, she'd been open with him about her family, about the effects of growing up under the rule of the Reverend. And even the times when she'd slipped into psychologist-mode talking about Tia, Meg hadn't been talking down to him, she'd been hiding in-securities of her own with it—something else she'd told him because she'd trusted him to grasp it, to understand.

So no, he realized as he blew away some of the sawdust to move on to another section of the table, he didn't actually think that Meg did have the same low opinion of him and his intelligence that Helene had had.

Besides, it wasn't Meg's style to look down on anyone. He knew that about her now. Meg was a fully-formed adult, and while the strict morals she'd been raised with might shadow some of her thinking, she was aware of the parts of her grandfather that could come out in her, and she took action to make sure she *didn't* end up anything like the Reverend.

Meg wasn't in some sort of stage that she would eventually evolve out of to become her true self. She was already her true self. And even now, after suffering something traumatic, when she *felt* as if more of her grandfather might be emerging in her, Meg wasn't merely letting that happen. She was dealing with it, doing everything she could to stop it.

So maybe, even in the light of day, there wasn't as much to put a damper on his feelings for her as he'd thought before.

But if that was true, then what?

What did he see for them? For himself and this woman who felt like the person he was meant to be with as surely as these two pieces of oak were meant to become this tabletop? This person who he felt more strongly about than he'd even felt about Helene?

Logan blew away most of the sawdust and ran his hand along the section of tabletop he'd been working on.

It was satin smooth. And that was all it took to remind him of Meg's skin, to make him want her so much he could hardly keep himself under control.

On his walk across the yard from the apartment at dawn this morning he'd counted how many hours would have to pass before Tia would be asleep again tonight, before Hadley would go to bed, and he could slip out to the garage apartment to see Meg again in private—the plan they'd devised before he'd left her.

But was that how the whole summer would be? Would they go on acting as if there was nothing between them during the day, just waiting for the moment when he could slip out like a thief in the night and go to her, to spend the hours of darkness with her, before he slinked back home again at dawn every morning?

The whole thing seemed a little cheap and sleazy.

And not the way he wanted things to be. Not with Meg.

He hated the idea of hiding, of sneaking, of slinking around. He wanted things to be out in the open.

But if they were, then Tia had to be factored in, too.

And if Tia was factored in, there was no way this could be a casual thing. There had to be some commitment. He had to know that there was a future to it.

Here he was thinking about a future together, about commitment.

About making Meg Tia's *step*mother…

That stopped his work completely.

He straightened up, stepped away from the table, and as he refocused his eyes, he thought, *The future. Commitment. Marriage?*

And somehow it didn't seem strange at all….

It was ten o'clock before Logan had been able to get to her apartment Monday night. After helping put Tia to bed and leaving Logan in the midst of a business phone call from his partner, Meg had had time to shower and wash her hair, to change into a pair of shorts and a bust-boosting camisole.

But when he'd finally arrived he hadn't done what she'd been assuming he would—what she'd been hoping he would—he hadn't whisked her back to the bed they'd both so reluctantly left behind this morning.

"You don't want to *defile* me?" Meg repeated with a laugh.

Instead, after a promising kiss that he'd cut short, he'd said he wanted to talk and had launched into something Meg wasn't sure she was following.

"That's what your grandfather would say I was doing, isn't it—defiling you?" Logan said.

They were standing not far into the apartment. Logan's arms were low around her waist, hooked at the hollow of her back. His jean-encased legs were brushing her bare ones, and she had her hands splayed against his T-shirted chest. And while she'd thought he'd been joking when he'd begun this conversation, she wasn't so sure now...

"*Defiling* does sound like a word my grandfather would use, yes," she answered. "But that's not how I feel."

"Maybe not yet. But what about months from now when this is all we've had—hiding up here every night, the rest of the time pretending that there isn't anything going on between us? Isn't that what you were afraid I wanted from you when I interviewed you—being Tia's nanny during the day and sleeping with me after-hours?"

That scenario had loomed in the back of her mind from the moment he'd left this morning. But every time it had crept to the forefront, Meg had chased it away with the thought of being where she was at that moment—here, alone with him. And because she hadn't wanted to think about anything *but* being here alone with him, she hadn't.

"It isn't as if the sneaking-around element hasn't occurred to me," Meg admitted even as she was breathing in the clean scent of him and reveling in the fact that she was finally in his arms again, where she'd wanted to be every minute of today. "You're right, that isn't a good thing," she conceded, "I just didn't want to think about it..."

"Well, I *did* think about it and I came to some realizations—first and foremost that that is *not* how I want things to be. That I want what we have out in the open, for anybody and everybody to see."

"So anybody and everybody can gossip about how we're sleeping together?"

"I don't want us to just be sleeping together, Meg," he announced.

That seemed like what he'd been leading up to but still Meg was so surprised that she didn't know what to say.

"I thought this through," he continued. "I thought about how I feel about you, how I feel when I'm with you, how I hate every minute that I'm *not* with you because it's like a part of me is missing—that's how I felt the whole damn time I was away last week. I thought about how I have this overwhelming sense that you and I are like two pieces of some grand-design puzzle that have finally come together. That isn't something we should have to do in any way that needs hiding. And when I put Tia into the mix, I realized that what I want is the whole package with you—the whole family package—"

"Oh, slow down!" Meg said, not confused anymore, but definitely alarmed.

Logan's arms tightened around her. "That's just it—I don't want to slow down. I don't see a reason to—"

"There are a whole lot of reasons to. Reasons why neither of us can make a decision like this right now—"

"I know it's quick—"

"It isn't *only* that it's quick," Meg insisted. "Decisions made in times of upheaval can be desperate attempts to regain control and not the right decisions at all."

"I'm not in upheaval."

"In the last few years your whole life has changed," Meg said, refuting that. "You became a father at a time when your marriage was crumbling, you got a divorce and ended up a single parent, you're in the process of moving your life and your business cross-country, and now you've just found out your ex-wife is getting married—"

"Desperation is *not* what I'm feeling," he said firmly and with conviction. "And this isn't some reaction to Helene getting married again—I couldn't care less about that, she's history for me. History I'm glad to have behind me."

"But that kind of thing can still throw you—"

"Maybe it *can*, but it hasn't. It doesn't have a damn thing to do with you and I."

"Everything has an effect, Logan."

"Well, the effect this time is that my marriage to Helene and my divorce from her let me know how right things are between you and I. And not only by comparison, but also because when I started to think about us having a future together I *didn't* freak out and think I'd rather be shot in the foot than go through anything like that again. I know you're different, I know what I feel for you is different, I know what we have is different."

He pulled her closer to him when he said that. But in the midst of shaking her head in denial Meg broke his hold and spun away from him to put some distance between them instead, facing him again only when she was several feet away where she hoped she could think more clearly.

"It may only *seem* right because it feels better than

the rejection and disillusionment and whatever else you've been feeling," she said then. "The same as this feels so much better to me than all the anxiety and fear and discontent I was feeling before. But that doesn't necessarily mean—"

"Jeez, don't do the psychologist thing," he said, sounding impatient. "I'm not a complicated person, Meg. I'm just an everyday guy who knows who and what he is. Who knows what he's feeling. And none of it needs to be analyzed or scrutinized for what it's masking. I'm just feeling what I'm feeling."

"I have to do the psychologist thing—"

"Because this freaks *you* out and when you get nervous you use it as armor. But don't. Not this time. This time just go with what you want."

"I don't know what I want!" Meg said with an edge of panic to her own tone. "That's why I came back to Northbridge in the first place—to sort things out. That's one of the reasons *I* can't make this kind of decision."

"Sure you can," he coaxed. "Just go with your instincts—think about last night, think about this morning when you kept pulling me back to bed, think about a couple of hours ago when we were with Tia and how it is every time the three of us are together—you can't tell me that you aren't already invested in us both. That it isn't so great you just want it to go on, too."

"It is great…" Meg said, wavering because what he said was true. More than he knew.

"You can argue down anything, Meg," Logan went on. "And yeah, what I'm proposing is built for it. But don't do it. Don't put the weight on the reasons why not, put the weight on what you feel, on what we have here."

An unfamiliar, foreign part of Meg urged her to just say okay. After all, more than once last night she'd pictured herself spending the rest of her life with this man. She'd wished for it.

But she'd also known that despite its appeal, the idea of actually trying to make that fantasy into reality at this point shouldn't even be entertained.

And even if she accepted Logan's claim that he knew himself and his feelings enough to trust that he could make a decision like this now, what Meg knew about herself was that at a time when she was questioning so many other things, making a decision of this magnitude was not wise. It was something she just couldn't do.

So she summoned every portion of her that was anything like her grandfather, stood straight and stiff, and said, "I can't do it, Logan. I just can't."

"You can do anything, Meg," he said as if he were encouraging her to take a dive off the high board. "There isn't a rule book here—"

"Don't use what I told you about Randy against me!"

"You said yourself that he was right, that you *had* played things too much by the book with him, that you disconnected from your own emotions. I'm just saying don't do that now, with us."

She hadn't thought she'd regret that he listened so intently to what she said but at that moment she did.

Logan continued, his voice lower. "You did this disconnecting thing with that other guy because you *weren't* really in that relationship with him whole-heartedly, because deep down you *didn't* have the kind of feelings for him that you should have had in order to marry him. Is that what you're telling me now? About me? About what we have together?"

"No!" she said without having to think about it. "I'm just telling you that we can't ignore—"

"We can ignore anything we want to ignore. There's nothing here but you and me and what we want and what we don't want. That's it. That's all there is. So either you want a future with me, or you don't."

"It isn't just black and white, Logan!"

"It is if you let it be."

"I can't let it be."

"You can if you let go of the rest, Meg. That's what you came here to do—to let go, to loosen up. So do it."

But everything she knew screamed at that unfamiliar impulsive portion of her that was tempted, screamed that to make a life-altering decision on a whim was just asking for trouble. Screamed that there was a child involved. A child who could get caught up in this. Who could get hurt…

"I can't let go of the rest because I know there's validity to it. And I also know that with Tia involved…" She shook her head. "There's all the more reason not to just let ourselves get carried away."

"Too late for that!" Logan nearly shouted.

But Meg merely shook her head again.

Logan sighed, jammed his hands into his rear pockets and slung his weight to jut out one hip. "So what do we do? This?" he demanded with a nod to the space around them. "Play we-just-work-together all day and then sneak up here for the nights?"

She knew that would never work. She'd known it before, which was why she'd avoided thinking about it every time it had weaseled its way into her head today. But now that he'd forced her to confront it, she had to.

"That isn't what you want to do and it isn't what I want to do, either," Meg nearly whispered.

But she also knew that there was no way she was going to be able to rewind the clock and take this back to a time when she could maintain even a semblance of control with him. If she stayed, this was where they would end up. If she even found somewhere else to live and just came out to be Tia's nanny, this would still be where she and Logan would end up because she wanted him too much for this *not* to be where they ended up…

"I think I just have to leave, Logan," she nearly whispered. "I'm sorry. I hate that you'll be left hanging when it comes to Tia—"

"Then don't do it," he said as if he couldn't believe what she was saying, as if everything in him wanted not to.

But Meg merely shook her head again and continued with what she'd been about to say. "I'll pack up tonight and talk to Tia in the morning so she'll have some closure before I go."

Logan's pale blue eyes bored into her as he took a turn shaking his head. But the longer he went on looking at her, the more anger appeared in his handsome face.

Then, as if he couldn't trust himself to say another word, he stormed out of the apartment.

And even though Meg was convinced that she'd

made the choice she needed to make, the emptiness that
flooded her once he was gone left her sorrier than she'd
ever been in her life that she'd had to make it.

Chapter Twelve

By eight o'clock the next morning Meg's things were stacked beside the apartment door waiting for her to load them into her car.

She'd showered, pulled her hair into a geyserlike ponytail at her crown, and applied some makeup to conceal what a miserable night she'd spent packing and crying. She wore jeans and a plain gray hoodie that zipped up the front.

But now the time had come for her to take her final walk across the yard to the main house to say goodbye to Tia.

And as much as she wanted to get it over with, somehow she couldn't force her feet to move.

Instead she was standing at the window that allowed her to look in that direction, wondering how she was going to get through this.

It wasn't as if she hadn't said goodbye to any number

of kids—some she'd done lengthy work with and become very attached to. But no matter how difficult it had been, she'd always managed to buck up and do it.

And yet with Tia, she just couldn't make herself.

Of course she hadn't been Tia's therapist, she'd been her nanny. And while she was always careful not to blur the line between therapist and parent, she knew she'd allowed that to happen to the line between being the nanny and being the mom.

Now she was paying the price for that.

And what if Tia did, too?

She hated that thought. Tia already had a mother who had abandoned her, who couldn't even visit her without being cold and critical. The last—the very last—thing Meg wanted was to be the second person in the three-year-old's life to leave her behind.

But that was what she'd opted to do and she knew she had to do it.

She just didn't want to. She didn't want to leave Tia. She most certainly didn't want to leave Logan…

Tears threatened again but Meg blinked them away. It wasn't as if they helped. This whole thing was tearing her apart and nothing made that any better.

Nothing except the thought of not following through with it.

Just go with what you want this time…

Logan's words kept repeating themselves in her mind, haunting her, tempting her.

But she had reasons not to go with what she wanted. Legitimate reasons. It was just that those reasons— strong as they were—weren't strong enough to actually put her into motion. And as a result she was stuck right where she was.

She was stuck to that spot at the window. Not doing what she knew she should be doing. Wondering how it was possible for her heart to be in such total disagreement with her head...

As she went on staring at the back of Logan's house, Tia opened the screen door, bounding out onto the deck in shorts, a flowered T-shirt and stockinged feet, her blond curls bouncing as if they were on springs. Harry and Max were fast on her heels and the sight of the three-year-old and her puppies almost made Meg cry again.

Did he tell you I'm leaving?

Tia seemed as carefree as ever and Meg was glad to see that. One way or another, the child wasn't upset.

Glad and also slightly hurt to think that Logan might have told Tia and that Tia cared as little as she cared when her neglectful mother left her behind.

But maybe Logan hadn't told her...

As Meg watched, Tia took the dogs' hairbrush out of a basket that held some of the puppies' things and began to attempt to groom the rambunctious animals. It was comical to see the dogs outwitting the three-year-old, and Meg couldn't help smiling even as it brought more tears to her eyes. But again she refused to let them fall.

Then Logan came out onto the deck, too.

And there was no stopping the hot, salty grief from trailing down her cheeks.

How could she cry and yearn for him all at once? Or was she crying *because* she was yearning for him so much and had denied herself?

She was afraid to answer that, instead putting her willpower into staunching the flow before she used a tissue she took from a nearby counter to dab at her face and eyes. All while keeping Logan in view.

He was wearing torn jeans and a blue chambray shirt that he often wore to work. The shirttails were untucked; the sleeves were rolled to his elbows. He was carrying a pair of Tia's tennis shoes that he took with him when he went to sit on the edge of the deck.

Wearily? Or was she misinterpreting the way he sort of deflated there? Meg wasn't sure. Although she did know that there had been lights on in his house all night long so she doubted he'd had any more sleep than she had.

But tired or not, a single dad still had duties and he began to use a stick to scrape dried mud off the bottom of the tennis shoes. All the while Tia went on futilely attempting to brush the dogs behind him.

And Meg thought: *There they are, and here I am...*

Alone with her certainty that she was right. That she knew best. That Logan was wrong...

He hadn't *really* been wrong, though, she had to admit.

He'd been right about how terrific the two of them were together. So terrific that Meg had begun to feel as if being with him was the only time she was totally alive. So terrific that every minute she wasn't with him she'd felt as if she were swimming against the tide to get to him again. So terrific that his every touch had energized her and merely the sight of him stirred a craving for him strong enough to almost make her groan even now.

And he'd been right about other things, too.

He'd been right about how terrific things were whenever they were both with Tia. How much fun it had been to take care of the little girl in tandem. How great it had been to share the joy of her as if she belonged to them both. They'd even been in sync when it came to disciplining and reprimanding her, when it came to parenting styles.

A voice inside of Meg was screaming for her to run to them, to pick up where she and Logan had left off last night before those stupid legitimate reasons of hers had ruined everything…

So he was right but she'd let her reasons ruin things? Was that really what she'd done? she asked herself. Had she overruled him as if she knew more than he did?

Maybe. But she thought her reasons were legitimate.

Things with Logan *had* happened fast.

She was just coming out of a rough time in her life.

And Logan *was* just coming out of a rough time in his and making a lot of changes in response.

Those were the facts and they worried her.

Just then Tia gave up trying to brush the puppies, attacked her father from behind with a bear hug around his neck, and a laughing Logan flipped her over his head to lay her across his lap and tickle her.

And the way Meg felt just watching them was enough to make all of her reasons—legitimate or otherwise—drift away like smoke. Leaving her with only her feelings bringing her to a decision.

Yoo-hoo, Logan, could you come up here a minute? she considered calling to him.

But she couldn't just do that, either.

So how was she going to get him up there?

Hadley?

Maybe she could call Hadley.

And hope that Hadley hadn't been up all night listening to Logan rehash every detail of what had happened, that Hadley hadn't spent the night consoling her brother and thinking the worst of her...

But it was the only thing Meg could think to do.

So she picked up her cell phone and dialed the other woman's number, willing Hadley not to think too badly of her if Hadley did know what she'd done...

Meg wasn't sure how long it might be before Logan came to the apartment after her phone call to his sister. With that uncertainty, she ignored the urge to try to find a change of clothes and merely took her hair down from its ponytail to brush it, and refined the makeup she'd applied earlier—camouflaging the damage done by her last bout of tears when she'd first seen Logan through the window.

Still, when the knock came on the apartment door half an hour later, she wished she was wearing something sexy and alluring that would aid her cause. As it was, the best she could do was lower the zipper on the hoodie by a few inches, and even then she was careful not to show cleavage because she didn't want to be too obvious or risk any more of her pride than she already was.

With her hand on the knob, she took a deep breath and exhaled in hopes that she would at least appear calm. Then she opened the door, grateful that her vague request that Hadley watch Tia and send Logan to the apartment had been met.

Logan didn't seem happy to be there, though. His handsome face was drawn, he looked more tired close-up than when she saw him sitting on the edge of the deck, and he didn't spare her more than a split-second glance before his eyes went to the suitcases and boxes beside the door—as if he couldn't stand the sight of her...

"Do you need help getting this stuff to your car?" he asked, apparently guessing that that was why she'd asked him to come.

"I hope not," Meg said softly. Some of her courage was waning but she pushed through and added, "I was hoping maybe we could talk—on a scale of one to ten with ten being that you'd like to see me hung by my thumbs from the barn roof, how mad would you say you are at me?"

As if he were assessing how best to haul her things out of there, he still hadn't let his gaze move away from them. But now he did, slowly pivoting his handsome head in her direction and raising his hands to his hips.

And for the first few moments that his pale blue eyes were on her, she thought that if there had been a fifteen on her mad-scale he would have chosen that.

But then he shook his head and said, "If this is some closure exercise to begin the healing or for some other psycho-babble reason, skip it."

Or maybe he would choose seventeen...

"That isn't what this is," Meg said, fearing more and more that she'd done irreversible damage.

"Then what is it?" he demanded.

"Maybe you could come all the way in and close the door?" she suggested since he had yet to cross the threshold.

He seemed disinclined to do that but after a moment he did it anyway, shutting the door and then leaning back against it, this time crossing his arms over his broad chest.

Confronted with Logan's obvious—and understand-able—anger with her, Meg wasn't sure what the best way to proceed might be. And she was too nervous for any of her work skills to kick in. Plus she was begin-ning to think that if this endeavor was going to blow up in her face she'd rather get to that part fast, so she said, "I don't want to go…"

He arched an eyebrow at her. "I'm not the one who said you had to."

"I know. But…" There was just no easy way to eat crow…

"I was wrong," Meg finally blurted out. "I was wrong and you were right, and I was stupid and pigheaded and stubborn and closed-off and blind and—"

"Wow," he said as the other eyebrow shot up, joining the first one. "And here I just thought you were scared."

"That, too," she confessed, feeling slightly better because while he might have said that with some resigned acceptance, he hadn't said it with any malice.

"I know a lot in theory," she continued then. "And I'm not saying any of it is worthless or unfounded or should be ignored because most of the time it has merit, but—"

"You're talking like a textbook—why don't you just relax and tell me what you have to say?" he said as if he were attempting to calm her down.

But his tone was warmer than it had been, his expres-sion wasn't as forbidding, and that helped.

"Sometimes you have to throw the book out the window," Meg said. "Sometimes no matter how fast it's happened, or under what kind of circumstances, or even if the timing isn't perfect—" she shrugged, "—it really is just the feelings that have to rule because the feelings are a six-hundred-pound gorilla in the room and they won't let you get past them."

And her eyes were welling up again for no reason she could fathom, and she was blinking like crazy to keep from crying again.

Which was when Logan pushed off the door and came to wrap his arms around her, to pull her against him and hold her head to his chest with one of those big hands that felt so, so good…

He dropped his forehead to the top of her head then and said in a quiet, emotional voice of his own, "On a scale of one to ten with ten being petrified, how afraid was I that you were never going to realize that?"

Meg laughed and that was what actually kept her from crying again. "So I wasn't the only one scared?"

"Of different things, but yeah, you weren't the only one scared."

"I'm sorry," she said then, her own arms around him, her hands splayed against that magnificent back. "It wasn't that you weren't what I wanted all along. It wasn't that being a mom to Tia wasn't what I wanted all along. It was just that I thought—"

"I know what you thought and it doesn't matter as long as you don't think it anymore."

Meg let go of him enough to veer backward slightly, to peer up at him. "I still think it," she admitted with a laugh. "It just doesn't change what I want and what I want is—"

"Me," he said with so much cocksureness that it made her laugh again.

But her heart was too full and she was too relieved that this was working out the way it was to do anything but agree with him and feed his show of ego. "Yes, what I want is you."

"More than your career?" he asked then, testing.

"More than my career in Denver," she qualified.

She'd thought about that part of this while she'd waited for him, and she'd admitted to herself that she didn't really care if she returned to her work at the hospital, that maybe the time for a change had come even before this and that that was why she'd needed to get away this summer. Which she told Logan now.

"I think I can still work here, though—there's the school, the hospital, there's the home for disturbed kids that's reopened. I think that offering my services on a case-by-case basis at any one of those will keep me busy enough. But not *too* busy…"

Logan smiled down at her, warmly, softly now. "I love you, Meg," he said for the first time.

"I love you, too," she could respond without a single doubt.

"And that's all that matters."

"Maybe sometimes it is," she conceded.

He kissed her then, his mouth coming to hers in a deep, deep kiss right from the start that bridged the gap that had separated them and reconnected them on a whole new level.

A deep, deep kiss that didn't have far to go to ignite passion in them both.

Logan's hands rose into her hair, holding her head to that kiss as his mouth opened over hers and his tongue rekindled some hotter, sexier things. Things that Meg welcomed and helped to flourish.

And then clothes began to come off and hands and

mouths found unveiled parts of each other's bodies that they'd learned well during their one night together, recalling what each of them liked, reawakening hunger and need in the blink of an eye.

Turning round and round, they crossed the short distance to the bed Meg had made and, naked by the time they reached it, Logan eased her down onto the quilt.

Maybe the thought that this might not have ever happened again spurred them on, but little more was called for before Logan found his way into Meg, before he took them both to a simultaneous peak that, when it subsided, had sapped every last drop of energy from them both.

Lying in those arms she knew she would have missed forever, Meg wilted and willingly went along when he rolled to his back and took her with him to lie on top of him, his chest her pillow.

"Go ahead, try and live without *that!*" he challenged then, once again cocky.

"Forget it, you're mine from here on, anytime I say," Meg countered the same way.

Logan laughed, a low, raspy sound that rumbled beneath her. "I'm just gonna be your sex slave?"

"Maybe."

"Uh-uh," he decreed. "I'm making an honest woman out of you whether you like it or not. I need a wife, my daughter needs a mother—"

Tia...

"Did you tell her I was leaving?" Meg asked, her alarm instantly turning off the tone of teasing.

"No," Logan answered. "I couldn't. I could hardly think of it myself, let alone tell anybody."

"Even Hadley?"

"Even Hadley. I figured that until you actually drove off, I wasn't saying anything."

Relieved, Meg returned to their teasing. "You just didn't think I'd do it, did you?"

"I didn't think I'd be able to stand it if you did," he answered quietly, seriously. Then, in a lighter note, he said, "Now tell me you'll marry me even though it might not be psychologically sound."

Meg laughed. "I'll marry you, even though *you* may not be psychologically sound," she teased.

"Better strong of body than mind," he joked in return, holding her tighter and flexing against her.

Still, regardless of how strong of body he was, their recent stress and lack of sleep was catching up with them both.

"What do you say we have a nap and then go tell Tia and Hadley what's going on?" Logan suggested then.

"I say yes," Meg agreed.

Logan rolled a half roll so that they were on their sides, his arms making sure she didn't get away from him, his chin resting on her head.

"I love you, Meg," he said again, as if he just wanted to.

"I love you, too, Logan," she whispered back.

As she listened to the steady beat of his heart, the way his breathing was growing slower, she was thinking of the days, the weeks, the years to come. Of being his wife and Tia's mom.

And a rush of happiness washed all through her to let her know as surely as she knew her name that allowing her feelings for Logan, for Tia, to be her guiding light had been exactly the right way to go.

* * * * *

*Harlequin Intrigue top author Delores Fossen
presents a brand-new series of
breathtaking romantic suspense!*
TEXAS MATERNITY: HOSTAGES
The first installment available May 2010:
THE BABY'S GUARDIAN

Shaw cursed and hooked his arm around Sabrina.

Despite the urgency that the deadly gunfire created, he tried to be careful with her, and he took the brunt of the fall when he pulled her to the ground. His shoulder hit hard, but he held on tight to his gun so that it wouldn't be jarred from his hand.

Shaw didn't stop there. He crawled over Sabrina, sheltering her pregnant belly with his body, and he came up ready to return fire.

This was obviously a situation he'd wanted to avoid at all cost. He didn't want his baby in the middle of a fight with these armed fugitives, but when they fired that shot, they'd left him no choice. Now, the trick was to get Sabrina safely out of there.

"Get down," someone on the SWAT team yelled from the roof of the adjacent building.

Shaw did. He dropped lower, covering Sabrina as best he could.

There was another shot, but this one came from a rifleman on the SWAT team. Shaw didn't look up, but he heard the sound of glass being blown apart.

The shots continued, all coming from his men, which meant it might be time to try to get Sabrina to better cover. Shaw glanced at the front of the building.

So that Sabrina's pregnant belly wouldn't be smashed against the ground, Shaw eased off her and moved her to a sitting position so that her back was against the brick wall. They were close. Too close. And face-to-face.

He found himself staring right into those sea-green eyes.

How will Shaw get Sabrina out?
Follow the daring rescue and the heartbreaking
aftermath in THE BABY'S GUARDIAN
by Delores Fossen,
available May 2010 from Harlequin Intrigue.

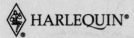

HARLEQUIN®

American ★ Romance®

LAURA MARIE ALTOM

The Baby Twins

Stephanie Olmstead has her hands full raising
her twin baby girls on her own. When she runs
into old friend Brady Flynn, she's shocked to find
herself suddenly attracted to the handsome airline
pilot! Will this flyboy be the perfect daddy—
or will he crash and burn?

**Babies
&
Bachelors
USA**

"LOVE, HOME & HAPPINESS"

www.eHarlequin.com

HAR75309

HARLEQUIN
Ambassadors

Want to share your passion for reading Harlequin® Books?

Become a Harlequin Ambassador!

Harlequin Ambassadors are a group of passionate and well-connected readers who are willing to share their joy of reading Harlequin® books with family and friends.

You'll be sent all the tools you need to spark great conversation, including free books!

All we ask is that you share the romance with your friends and family!

You'll also be invited to have a say in new book ideas and exchange opinions with women just like you!

To see if you qualify* to be a Harlequin Ambassador, please visit www.HarlequinAmbassadors.com.

*Please note that not everyone who applies to be a Harlequin Ambassador will qualify. For more information please visit www.HarlequinAmbassadors.com.

Thank you for your participation.

BAP09BPA

HARLEQUIN *Presents*

Bestselling Harlequin Presents® author

Lynne Graham

introduces

VIRGIN ON HER WEDDING NIGHT

Valente Lorenzatto never forgave Caroline Hales's
abandonment of him at the altar. But now he's
made millions and claimed his aristocratic Venetian
birthright—and he's poised to get his revenge.
He'll ruin Caroline's family by buying out their
company and throwing them out of their mansion…
unless she agrees to give him the wedding night
she denied him five years ago….

**Available May 2010
from Harlequin Presents!**

INTRIGUE

BESTSELLING
HARLEQUIN INTRIGUE® AUTHOR

DELORES FOSSEN

PRESENTS AN ALL-NEW
THRILLING TRILOGY

TEXAS MATERNITY: HOSTAGES

When masked gunmen take over the maternity ward at a San Antonio hospital, local cops, FBI and the scared mothers can't figure out any possible motive. Before long, secrets are revealed, and a city that has been on edge since the siege began learns the truth behind the negotiations and must deal with the fallout.

LOOK FOR

THE BABY'S GUARDIAN, May
DEVASTATING DADDY, June
THE MOMMY MYSTERY, July

Love Inspired

Former bad boy Sloan Hawkins is back in
Redemption, Oklahoma, to help keep his aunt's
cherished garden thriving and to reconnect with the
girl he left behind, Annie Markham. But when he
discovers his secret child—and that single mother
Annie never stopped loving him—he's determined
that a wedding will take place in the garden
nurtured by faith and love.

REDEMPTION
RIVER

Where healing flows...

Look for

The Wedding Garden
by Linda Goodnight

*Available May 2010
wherever you buy books.*

www.SteepleHill.com

Steeple
Hill®

LI87595

REQUEST YOUR FREE BOOKS!
2 FREE NOVELS PLUS 2 FREE GIFTS!

SPECIAL EDITION
Life, Love and Family!

YES! Please send me 2 FREE Silhouette® Special Edition® novels and my 2 FREE gifts (gifts are worth about $10). After receiving them, if I don't wish to receive any more books, I can return the shipping statement marked "cancel." If I don't cancel, I will receive 6 brand-new novels every month and be billed just $4.24 per book in the U.S. or $4.99 per book in Canada. That's a saving of 15% off the cover price! It's quite a bargain! Shipping and handling is just 50¢ per book.* I understand that accepting the 2 free books and gifts places me under no obligation to buy anything. I can always return a shipment and cancel at any time. Even if I never buy another book from Silhouette, the two free books and gifts are mine to keep forever.

235/335 SDN E5RG

Name	(PLEASE PRINT)	
Address		Apt. #
City	State/Prov.	Zip/Postal Code

Signature (if under 18, a parent or guardian must sign)

Mail to the **Silhouette Reader Service:**
IN U.S.A.: P.O. Box 1867, Buffalo, NY 14240-1867
IN CANADA: P.O. Box 609, Fort Erie, Ontario L2A 5X3

Not valid for current subscribers to Silhouette Special Edition books.

Want to try two free books from another line?
Call 1-800-873-8635 or visit www.morefreebooks.com.

* Terms and prices subject to change without notice. Prices do not include applicable taxes. N.Y. residents add applicable sales tax. Canadian residents will be charged applicable provincial taxes and GST. Offer not valid in Quebec. This offer is limited to one order per household. All orders subject to approval. Credit or debit balances in a customer's account(s) may be offset by any other outstanding balance owed by or to the customer. Please allow 4 to 6 weeks for delivery. Offer available while quantities last.

Your Privacy: Silhouette is committed to protecting your privacy. Our Privacy Policy is available online at www.eHarlequin.com or upon request from the Reader Service. From time to time we make our lists of customers available to reputable third parties who may have a product or service of interest to you. If you would prefer we not share your name and address, please check here. ☐

Help us get it right—We strive for accurate, respectful and relevant communications. To clarify or modify your communication preferences, visit us at www.ReaderService.com/consumerschoice.

SSE10R